'I love reading Sarah Govett.'

Dame Emma Thompson

'This is a highly original dystopian novel with a thrilling plot and memorable characters you really root for. Thought-provoking and at times terrifying, this book had me gripped from the start and I couldn't put it down. Highly recommended for fans of *The Hunger Games*.'

Sarah J Harris, author of
The Colour of Bee Larkham's Murder

'Sarah Govett has written one of the most intriguing and exciting dystopian thrillers I have read in a long time! This book grabs you from page one and holds on until the last word. A fascinating world filled with beautifully written characters.'

Ben Oliver, author of *The Loop*

'Addictive and compelling – I absolutely love this book.'
Louisa Reid, author of *Wrecked* and *Gloves Off*

for Noa, Alba and Ned

WE GO ON FOREVER

Sarah Govett

First published in 2021
by Marotte Books Ltd
51 York Avenue, London SW14 7LQ

www.marottebooks.com
Text © Sarah Govett 2021

A CIP catalogue record of this book is available from the British Library.

Print ISBN 978-1-9161526-8-7

Typeset by Elaine Sharples
Printed and bound by PULSIO SARL

Cover design by Liam Relph

ARTHUR

The sky is a rich Matisse-blue and I tilt up my chin to catch the midday sun. I've always found September sun to be the most precious – summer's imminent departure adding an immeasurable sweetness. It's a day for picnics. For lounging in short sleeves. Not for doctors' surgeries. Not for results.

A voice calls my name, and I turn away from the open window, back to the reception. For a second I catch my reflection in the gilded mirror that hangs above the desk and I scrutinise my face as a stranger might. Symmetrical, unlined. I haven't noticed it age in the last two years. The stranger would most likely guess it to be some years younger than the nineteen it is now.

Dr Peters' secretary ushers me through to his office. I decline her offer of refreshments.

The MRI results are displayed on a screen in the centre of the room, awaiting my arrival. Twelve cross-sections through my brain. A four by three grid. There – second from the top in the middle – a white circle lurks in the right hemisphere. A UFO sighting in an otherwise foggy skyline. I shut the door behind me and Dr Peters plasters on the special sort of smile he reserves for patients holding Level One insurance policies. I sit and the smile widens even further in recognition of my status. As heir to the M.A.D.E. conglomerate, I get to see a lot of teeth.

Dr Peters embarks upon small talk, a tapestry of medical and societal aspects interwoven. How am I feeling? How is my father? Are the headaches worsening? Did I manage much sailing over the summer? Did I try this great new seafood place? He'll give me the name of the owner – another patient of his; it's hellish to get a table otherwise. And the balance problems?

'How long?' I ask, cutting him short. I need the facts. I'm meeting Tommy for tennis at two and I don't want to be late for the second time running. I might not be at the top of my game but I can still manage to hit a ball.

'Four to six weeks,' Dr Peters replies, his smile taking on a frozen quality. I think of icebergs and the Norwegian Fjords.

A month.

I sit and try to absorb the information.

Dr Peters picks up a long, thin stick and starts pointing at the screen, punctuating each comment with a sharp staccato rap. The ingratiating smile is gone and he seems more natural, calmer; happier hiding behind a medical lexicon of obfuscation.

'The results of the biopsy show the tumour to be

malignant. The MRI cross-sections here *RAP!* and here *RAP!*, show it to be present in the cerebellum, hence the balance control issues. The size indicates a grade 3 tumour, meaning growth is rapid and recurrence after surgery a distinct probability. I would currently place you at 90 on the Karnofsky Performance Status Scale as you are only experiencing minor symptoms, but this is likely to deteriorate rapidly in the next four to six weeks. In my opinion, you should be looking to transition in the next fortnight to ensure no further damage to brain tissue and to prevent potential permanent memory loss and cognitive impairment.'

Two weeks. Damn. I'm supposed to be meeting Parachute to discuss final details on the 25th. I'd still be adjusting then.

There's a sound of rapid tapping. An object being repeatedly struck at a frequency that makes my nerves tingle. Where's it coming from? My eyes scan the floor and alight on my right foot. It's knocking against the metal leg of the chair. I stare at it, detached. An observer.

'Mr Easton, is everything all right?' The smile is gone and Dr Peters is looking at me, brow furrowed in concern. He isn't used to this sort of behaviour. Tommy says he only really takes on Level One patients now. Dealing with lower insurance levels, not to mention the DMWs (*Dead Men Walking*, as Tommy calls them), and their tiresome anxieties can really interfere with one's golf.

I don't answer him immediately. I'm locked inside my head.

'Mr Easton…?'

His voice has a slight tremor. I'm such a fool. He's on alert now. He'll report back to Father for sure.

'It's fine, thanks. I'm fine. I'll contact the Transition Centre straight away.'

I stand and head towards the door. I'm getting a headache. One of the bad ones. I don't know why this is affecting me so much. This body has only hosted me for two years, the previous one lasted seven and I felt nothing. Maybe it was a mistake to choose one that was too similar to my Original. Same age: seventeen at time of transition. Same build: broad but not overdeveloped; 'a swimmer's body', the breakdown had said. Same colouring: tanned skin, light brown hair that regains its blonde in summer. Same eyes even – green with flecks of yellow. Too many sames. It's harder when it fails. I'll choose something different next time. Get less attached.

I think I'll cancel Tommy after all. I'm not really in the mood for tennis.

ALBA

I'm sitting next to Curly, willing the Morning Meeting to end. Eventually the screen recedes and the Supervisor twists up the corners of her mouth in a poor imitation of a smile.

'Now, some good news,' she says, trying to sound light and enthusiastic. It doesn't suit her. 'Another one of you has been chosen as an Apprentice. Tomorrow they will travel to the Research City to help their Mentor with the crucial work of cleansing the Wilderness. Praise the Creator.'

'Praise the Creator,' we all mumble back, but no one's putting any effort into it. We're all too busy scanning the room, seven hundred heartbeats stopped in anticipation. *Who is it? Who's been chosen?*

'Will F3526 please approach the stage.'

It takes a second to register who she's talking about. The Creator assigns us our numbers. To deviate from them is heresy even though nearly everyone apart from the Supervisor and the Guardians does it.

My heart stops as Curly shoots me a quick look of astonishment and then stands up and starts to edge forward through a sea of applause. Curly. *Curly.* 'No, no, NO!' I inwardly scream. I know I should be happy for her, rejoicing too, but all I can think is, *Please don't take my friend. Not yet. I'm going to miss her too much.* I know I'm being selfish and I should ask the Creator for forgiveness, but still; it's Curly. And she's been my best friend, my only proper friend, since, well, since forever.

I don't know why it comes as such a surprise. I always knew she'd be one of the first of our year to be chosen. She's off-the-scale clever, mastering Further Maths and Physics while the rest of us were still groping around with Newton and his apple. And she's beautiful. Stunning, even. She has this flawless, dark-brown skin and black curls that just sort of tumble around her face. And when she moves, she kind of glides. All the boys just stare at her. The Guardians too. Ever since she turned fourteen.

The younger ones clap with barely contained excitement. Eligibility for selection starts at sixteen, so to be chosen at seventeen is an incredible honour and it gives them hope that it could be them soon. It's different with the older ones. The ones in their late twenties. If they aren't chosen by thirty they'll be transferred to a different Home. Their applause is mechanical and jealousy palpably radiates off them. If you could see them on a different plane, their eyes would be leaping out at you, shining the brightest green. Me, I just taste bile rising at the back of my throat.

6

Eventually Curly reaches the foot of the stage and then climbs the steps to stand at the Supervisor's side.

'Congratulations F3526, you've been selected as the next Apprentice. You are to report to the office tomorrow morning at seven. I hope the rest of you take inspiration from her deportment, intelligence and dedication.'

The Supervisor doesn't hug Curly, or even smile at her in any way. She just watches her face – no doubt for evidence of the required level of gratitude.

'Thank you. Praise the Creator,' Curly replies, her voice measured and lyrical as she gives the obligatory response. But she isn't OK. I know she isn't. Even before she trips on the last step as she descends from the stage.

ARTHUR

The call comes from Dr Peters' office as I'm parking in front of my apartment building. He's terribly apologetic but he's forgotten to give me the latest immunisation boost. He needs me to return to the surgery immediately.

'Can't it wait?' I ask tersely. After all, I'm going to be transitioning in a fortnight. How much will it really help in the interim?

'I'm afraid it can't,' he replies, his voice hand-wringingly contrite. 'Company policy. Your father was very clear.'

The fear in his voice is palpable. Offend Father and your job is at risk. Your Level One status suddenly negotiable.

I sigh and restart the engine.

At least I don't need to see Dr Peters again. The injection is given by a new nurse in a side room. She's pretty in an understated way, with strong cheekbones and a generous mouth, and her brown eyes knit together in concentration as she swabs the skin at the top of my left arm. The diligence of someone new to the job. Her hands shake slightly as she fills the needle from a vial and my heart goes out to her. She's wearing gloves but no lower face mask. A calculated risk. A mask would be safer but it's also alienating so she would never become truly popular with her clients who are used to uncovered faces. To smiles. And a popular nurse can do very well. A few have made such an impression on high-profile patients that they've ended up with sponsored Level One status.

'This may hurt a little,' she suggests as she produces a needle.

I smile, a little patronizingly, I admit.

She holds the skin taut and inserts the needle and I gasp in spite of myself. I've had enough injections to know to expect a short, sharp scratch sensation. This is completely different. It hurts. It hurts like hell.

I brusquely take the plaster she offers but it does little to stem the trickle of blood that's seeping from the hole. She needs to be careful. I'm not going to say anything – I don't want her on my conscience – but others will. And unless she improves her technique, she'll garner a score of complaints and get fired. Her shot at being more than a DMW lost forever.

ALBA

We're the only ones in the dorm – everyone else is still at dinner. We're sitting on Curly's bed, folding her spare tunics, socks and underwear, ready to pack, when Guardian 17 comes in. Her short brown hair is savagely parted and tucked behind her ears and her thick arms test the seams of her dark blue uniform.

She takes one look at the pile of clothes then instructs us to put them back in the drawers again.

'They will be redistributed,' she says. 'You will be issued with new garments at the Research Centre. It saves them having to decontaminate the ones you take with you. You just need the one outfit for travel. It will be under your hazmat suit and protected.'

'Yes, Guardian,' Curly replies in a small voice.

'You may select a small number of mementos for your transfer bag to remind you of your time here. That's all.'

I think for a moment.

'But won't they get contaminated too during the journey?' I ask.

'No,' Guardian 17 replies curtly. 'The bag will be in a

different part of the vehicle and anyway, the radiation won't cling to it in the same way.'

I don't totally get this as surely radiation clings to all particles equally? But then again, I think we learnt once that alpha radiation gets blocked by paper, and beta radiation can't get through metal foil so maybe this was a bit like that? I open my mouth to ask more questions, but Curly catches my eye and glares me into silence. They don't like too many questions.

'F3526, you have a final task to complete this afternoon.' Guardian 17 produces some paper and a pen from a bag and puts them on the bed. The pages are covered in small, spidery writing, illegible unless you squint. 'You are to copy these pages. Each line twenty times. The writing is to look the same. Exactly the same.'

Curly looks at the pages and says nothing.

'Why?' The word escapes my lips before I'm even aware I'm saying it.

Guardian 17 stares at me in contempt. 'The Mentors require it,' she spits. 'Not that *you'll* ever meet them.' She mutters the last bit under her breath but it's still loud enough for me to hear and it cuts me inside.

Curly spends the next hour or so writing. The style is so hard to copy that she's concentrating intensely and her tongue is poking out of her mouth in effort. She looks hilarious and when I mention it, we both end up cracking up laughing and then the whole thing ends up taking another half hour. The final result isn't brilliant but it's good enough. Spidery, small and pretty illegible. Weird job done.

When Curly's finished the writing, I help her pack her transfer bag. It's grey canvas, exactly the same dimensions and fabric as the one sitting under my bed. Ready. For the day I'm chosen. If that ever comes. We made the bags in sewing last year. The first year we could have been selected. We were allowed to embroider on tiny details, patterns to personalise them. I sewed a small pink heart on mine. Curly embroidered a flower on hers. A rose. We saw one in a book in the library and she couldn't get over how beautiful it was. She gave the rose red petals and green leaves and for the last leaf she made the tip curl round and round as a kind of secret signature.

The day we made them we were so excited. I remember us hugging the finished products and imagining us being chosen and filling them. In our imagination it had always been together.

Now it's just Curly.

She doesn't take too long to choose what to take. First in goes a photo of the two of us, grinning at the camera. Guardian 9 (call-me-Rich-but-not-when-they're-around) gave it to her for her seventeenth Creation Day present. We're not supposed to keep photos and, anyway, they're never normally printed out. They're all supposed to be digital, serious, one-person shots to be added to our portfolios to show the Mentors. But he took this one of us when no one else was watching and later slipped it to her with a wink and a whisper. Curly looks stunning as always, whereas I look ridiculous. All features, no face. A massive toothy smile devouring my cheeks from below as my spreading-out flat nose attacks them from the side. I hope it was the result of a wide-angled lens. If I actually look like that, no Mentor is ever going to work with me. I don't think they have a huge need for gargoyles in the Research City.

Alongside the photo, Curly packs a clay vase I once made in Art. We swapped at the end of the lesson. Hers, which sits on my bedside table, is perfect – the clay smooth, the design elegant and intricate, the brushstrokes clean: poppies dancing in a meadow. Mine had collapsed on the turntable and then I'd smudged the butterflies I'd attempted to paint, so as a whole it resembles a molehill covered in a swarm of mutant insects. Curly says she'll treasure it forever.

Third and finally she adds a comb to tame her tight curls into obedience. 'If they see morning-me without it, they'll soon reverse their decision,' she laughs. 'I'll be the first Apprentice ever to be sent back again!' As if. Morning Curly is beautiful as is afternoon Curly as is evening Curly.

13

She zips up the bag and we sit either side of it. Our history. Our friendship, captured and condensed.

30cm by 20cm by 10cm.

* * *

Now we're lying in bed, Curly's head a metre from my own. Where it's always been. Guardian 9, call-me-Rich, says we've always been inseparable. Ever since we were created, just one day apart. That as a baby I'd sucked my thumb for comfort, and then one day he'd found me lying next to Curly, sucking her thumb instead.

'I'm going to miss you so much, Alba.' Curly's voice steals through the dark. She's called me Alba for ten years now. It started when we learnt about alabaster carvings in Culture. She said my skin's the exact same colour. Blinding white.

'Me too,' I whisper back, glad that she can't see the tears spilling down my cheeks. I have to be brave for her. Brave for the both of us. 'But it's a good thing, isn't it? Such an honour,' I continue, forcing my voice to stabilise, to switch from minor to major key. In doing so, I become weirdly upbeat. 'Hardly anyone gets chosen at seventeen. You'll be living in the Research City. Making a difference. Knowing you, you'll have figured out a way to cleanse the Wilderness in a couple of months. And I'm sure your Mentor will be kind and smart and teach you so much.'

14

'Thanks, Alba. I'm grateful,' she crosses herself quickly, 'don't get me wrong. And excited too. It's just I've never left this place, you know?' The words *never left you* weren't spoken, but hover between us, spectrally, nonetheless.

'Just don't forget about me, OK?' I choke out, all pretense at upbeat abandoned.

'Never.'

'And write. You have to. Everyone always promises to write and then gets so caught up in their exciting new life in the City that they don't bother.'

'I'll write.'

'Promise?'

'On the *Book of the Creator*.'

A silence nestles between us. It's comforting.

'Oh, and, Alba.' Curly's voice is more serious now. Tinged with urgency.

'Yes?'

'Work really hard, OK? You've got those English and Chemistry tests coming up. Ace it this time. And watch your deportment. You were hunching in your last video. You know the Mentors don't like hunching.'

'Revise. Don't hunch. Got it.'

'And no jokes. They don't like jokes. Or questions. You ask too many questions.'

'So, I basically need to totally change my personality?' I laugh.

'Yup, that's about it.' Curly echoes my laughter. Like with everything else, it's a prettier, daintier version. A tinkling bell to my tuba.

'You'll get picked soon, too, I know it.'

I hope she's right. By the Creator, I hope she's right. Then I can leave this place, leave the Supervisor and the Guardians and all their rules and move to the City and be with Curly again.

ARTHUR

It's raining as I approach Father's office. It's just before four. He's chosen the day and the time.

'Four sharp, Arthur,' said his clipped message on my phone. 'Don't be late.'

I ride the lift up to the eighth floor, my shoes leaving wet footprints on the marble tiles as I take a seat on the leather sofa facing his office.

He still keeps me waiting for twenty minutes before Linda, his secretary, buzzes me in. It's not like he was in a meeting that overran or anything. No awkward visitor who wouldn't leave. In fact, no one came in or out of his office at all during the twenty minutes – I was watching the door the whole time. It's just one of his forms of power play. Pathetic.

I enter, and my senses are hit as always by the strong smell of cigar smoke and furniture polish. They say that people retain the tastes of their Original. I've seen my father morph from white-haired man in his late fifties to a thirty-year-old bronzed Mediterranean type to the Swedish-looking, chisel-cheeked, mid-twenties man he is now, changing bodies before they expire just for the fun

17

of it, but the cigar smoke and furniture polish smell has remained throughout; an external constant. That and the bullying and the sense that I am and always will be a disappointment. Unnecessary.

There's a count of three before he deigns to look up.

'Ah, Arthur, come in, come in.'

I'm already in. I'm standing right there in front of him.

'You wanted to see me?' I'm in no mood for small talk. The headache still hasn't completely gone and my upper arm is still throbbing from the injection, the paracetamol not kicking in this time.

The smoke is starting to make me feel sick and Father must register for once as he stubs the end of the smouldering cigar into the ashtray on his desk.

'These things will be the death of me.' Cue raucous laughter. His own. The joke wasn't even funny the first time.

I say nothing so Father is forced to continue.

'Dr Peters called.' Of course he had. He was worried about my reaction and was covering his back. Protecting himself from his most valued client. In case I was like Mother. *Sensitive* they called her. *Weak-minded.* Bastards. She was saner than any of them. She was the only one who'd seen this life for exactly what it was.

'He said you hadn't taken the news well. Had *reacted* to the idea of transition.' He says it like I'd baulked at the idea of trying a new flavour of ice cream. *No son of mine … heir I don't need… just like his mother.* I can read the thoughts that flit across his forehead like a flip-book animation.

'No, it's fine. I'm fine.' Apparently my new mantra.

'Have you contacted the Transition Centre yet?'

I pause. I haven't. Why haven't I?

'Well, get on with it, Son. My company … *our* company invented this procedure. We can't be seen to be squeamish about using it now, can we? What sort of message would that project? HeathTech has been after our government licence for years. We can't give them any ammunition.'

As if HeathTech were a real concern. They stand no chance of getting the contract. The all-important Level Ones are happy. The Prime Minister, permanently upgraded to a Level One by virtue of his job, is happy. Everyone bar HeathTech's two representatives on the Companies Committee is happy, so a change of appointed government is fundamentally unlikely any time soon. It would take a seismic shift in opinion to topple the status quo. It would require the Committee members to vote against their own vested interests, and history suggests that people don't do that. They just come up with justifications for why they drew the lines in the sand in the first place.

My incredulity must show on my face as his pretense at calm, of fatherly concern evaporates and, instead, tiny bits of spittle start flying from the corners of his mouth.

'How hard can it be, for God's sake, Arthur? Contact the Centre. Organise a date for transition. Do it by a week on Friday, latest. I want you in Paris with me on the 25th. We have a big new potential investor to impress. They like families in France. They have fewer of them left over there.'

And there it is. The truth. It makes Father look good to have me around. The son of his Original. Shows him to be one of the first. When the elite still actually reproduced, as they didn't know the immortality project would work. When people thought they might need an heir to take over from them.

Now they don't. And here we are. A cluster of heirs who aren't being groomed to take over anything. An accessory who gets to play tennis and make their father look good in Paris.

I take a deep breath. Now's the time to tell him. I know he won't take it well but I have to. To emerge from his shadow for the sake of my sanity.

'I've been meaning to tell you, Father. I'm not coming to Paris.' I try to meet his eye but feel my voice starting to waver. Even after all these years he still has this effect on me. Makes me feel five years old again. I can't be distracted, so I switch the focus of my vision slightly so that it rests on his left earlobe. There's a mole there I haven't noticed before. A freckle possibly, gifted by summer. It's dead-centre, like an earring. It almost makes me smile. Probably the only homophobic man left on the planet looks like he's wearing an earring. As soon as he notices, he'll transition…

Focus. Tell him… 'I'm meeting Parachute on the 25th.'

Father is smiling now. Like it's all a big joke. Like I'm a big joke. Anger galvanises my voice.

'They've offered me a job.'

'You have a job.'

'I'll be heading up their vaccine research arm.'

'You're already head of vaccine research here.'

'Their position is properly funded.'

Father switches tack.

'The bacteria are mutating too fast for vaccination to be effective. You've seen it yourself. It'll never work.' The irony of it. How many times had Father been told his goal was unachievable? 'And anyway,' he continues, 'the present system functions. It even has its advantages.'

I know he's trying to goad me but I rise to the bait anyway.

'How can you say that? How can a system that leaves the majority weak and dying "function"?'

A slow smile spreads over Father's face.

'How do you think this majority would react if they suddenly regained their health and longevity? After years of suffering, of watching their family members die, how do you think they would thank you?'

21

I manage to say nothing this time. There's no point. He's deliberately provoking me. He knows how I feel. The sooner I'm out of this place and away from him the better.

'I'm taking the job.'

'No, Son.'

'I am.' I hear the petulant whinge in my tone and hate myself for it.

'They've withdrawn their offer.'

My left eyeball starts to vibrate. A barometric facial tic from childhood.

'Parachute called me as a courtesy to check that I was on board with you leaving M.A.D.E. I said that I wasn't. Your place is here, Arthur. It always will be. We fly on the 24th.'

He picks up a pen. Gold, embossed with a griffin. He's always had a thing for Greek myths. Imagines himself as a cross between an eagle and a lion, flying, roaring above the hordes.

'Don't forget tomorrow's AGM.'

He begins to sign the paperwork that's arranged in perfect parallel lines on his desk. The message is clear. *You're dismissed.*

I turn to leave, the rug seeming to rise towards me and my side colliding with the door frame on the way out. God, the headache's bad now. I'll ask Tommy if he's got something that can take the edge off. He usually does.

ALBA

We arrive outside the Supervisor's Office early. Curly presses her ear to the door. Silence. She knocks tentatively but gets no reply so we hover in the corridor, waiting for the Supervisor to turn up. Guardian 17 arrives and stands at a distance, waiting too, her hands tucked into her trouser pockets, biceps stretched. We don't say anything. There's nothing left to say, nothing we want to say with the beady eyes of Guardian 17 looking on anyway. She doesn't take them off us. Just keeps looking us up and down as if she had super-scanner X-ray lasers imbedded in them or something. Instead we hold hands and I feel Curly's pulse, unnaturally fast, jumping at the top of her wrist.

A door just along the corridor – the door to the lift to the basement – opens and we both tense up. But it's a false alarm. Just the weekly food delivery. Guardian 8 emerges, pushing a metal trolley on which huge sacks of oats, flour, rice, nuts and trays of tins are balanced. We're pretty self-sufficient here but can't grow everything. His whole body is straining from the weight, dark stains spreading out from his armpits like a chromatography experiment and sweat slicking down his thin blonde hair. The trolley squeaks as he pushes it away in the other direction – towards the kitchens. Our eyes don't follow him though. Instead we both stare at the lift door as it closes, knowing that it will soon be closing behind Curly too.

The sound of the Supervisor's footsteps ringing against the wooden floor of the corridor reaches us before she does and Curly switches on a smile and pulls back her shoulders. Anyone else would have thought that Curly was experiencing the correct emotions – happiness, pride, anticipation. But then no one else knows Curly like I do. The tiny dimple in her chin is wobbling, which it only does if she's really nervous. I know it's not really called a dimple. That you're supposed to say 'cleft' for a chin indentation. But cleft doesn't sound right; it's too masculine. And there's nothing masculine about Curly. So I say chin-dimple instead. Which means Curly has three dimples. One in either cheek and then the chin-dimple symmetrically below. Guardian call-me-Rich once called her face a Bermuda triangle. Said you can get lost in it.

'What's Bermuda?' I remember asking.

'A place,' he'd replied evasively.

'In the Wilderness?'

Guardian Rich had paused fractionally before nodding. There are so many places in the Wilderness. So many places we haven't studied yet.

'Right. F3526, are you ready?' the Supervisor's sharp tone pulls me back to the present.

Curly nods. I give her one final hug, squeezing and squeezing. I never want to let go.

'That's enough,' barks the Supervisor, and Guardian 17 pulls me away, looking like she's enjoying it.

'Follow me, F3526.' The Supervisor spins on her heels and heads to the lift door, pressing her finger to the access panel to summon the lift to take them to the basement. The basement is where the hazmat suits are kept. Where any visitors arrive and leave from. The departure point for new Apprentices. It's strictly out of bounds. The danger of contamination if a suit gets damaged in any way is too great.

I try to remain calm, quiet. The way a good future Apprentice might. But I can't.

'Good luck, Curly!' The words burst out my mouth and chase after her disappearing figure. They catch her as she's halfway through the door. Last minute she turns round and flashes me a killer smile.

My eyes are flooding with tears and I try to blink them away. We're going to be photographed later and my eyes swell up when I cry and I look properly ugly. No one will want to be my Mentor if they see me like that.

The bell for Morning Meeting rings, but I ignore it. All I can think is that I have to get to the field. Need to; in the same way that my lungs need to breathe and my heart needs to beat. To run to the top of the mound and stare at the road that snakes off into the Wilderness and towards the Research City beyond. To catch a glimpse of the car that takes Curly away.

I head towards the side corridor, planning to use the back stairs. I begin by tiptoeing but the adrenaline takes over and next thing I know my legs are clattering down the steps. Tears are blurring my vision and I don't see the Guardian coming up the other way until it's too late. We collide in a bundle of limbs.

'Watch out!' His voice is harsh and accusatory.

I look up and wipe the sleeve of my shirt across my face, readying myself for the inevitable barrage of abuse.

'Alba?' The voice softens and I relax. It's call-me-Rich. He looks concerned and tired, grey skin matching grey hair, the grey eyes behind his round glasses rimmed with red.

'I need to watch her go, sir.'

'No, Alba,' even his voice sounds drained. 'You need to come to the Morning Meeting.'

'But—'

'No buts. Now.' His voice is raised again and urgent. Even he doesn't understand. I don't have a choice. I'll live with the consequences. I feint to the right and then sprint to the left, taking the stairs three at a time. I can hear him coming after me, but I don't look back. At the bottom of the staircase I take a left, then it's a fifty-metre straight dash to the side door. It's got a push-bar catch and it's alarmed, but I don't let that stop me. Heart thumping in my ribcage, I shove the bar and I'm outside, gulping air. No time to stop, to catch my breath. The alarm screams as I pound round the gravel path that hugs the metal Fence. I pass the animal barns and vegetable patch and then I'm on the running track. I can't see anything out there yet as the metal's too high. When I reach the bottom of the mound, that's when I leave the track and start to climb, legs like pistons. Only at the top I stop, clutching my side. The morning's clear, so I have an uninterrupted view. The landscape stretches out in front of me like a rolled-out map; the road a tarmac river through it. From here it's impossible to see where the good land ends and the Wilderness begins. The border a question of degrees rather than something physical and fixed. I scan the road but there's no sign of a car. Nothing. I was too slow. I missed her. I'm too late.

I'm howling at the sky. Howling so loud that I don't hear Guardian Rich come up behind me. He touches my shoulder and I spin round, muscles tensing, adrenaline spiking again.

I'm ready to run, but he doesn't have a go at me. Doesn't grab me to take me inside. Just stares at me, red-rimmed eyes filled with concern.

'I missed her,' I say.

'I'm sorry,' he replies simply. And then hugs me. And I sob into his shoulder until I can cry no more.

27

ARTHUR

The foyer of M.A.D.E.'s Head Office is already swarming with shareholders. It always takes me a moment to get used to seeing this number of people gathered together in close proximity. It's not something you see normally. Not without masks, at any rate.

The AGM isn't due to start for another forty minutes, but I think people just really like being here. And it's not purely because of the towering silver breakfast platters that cover the side tables, although they shouldn't be entirely disregarded. You'd have thought that free food would lose its thrall when you've conquered death, but never underestimate the power of a mini-muffin basket or a smoked salmon vol-au-vent. I'm being flippant. It's more than that. They like the building. They come here to worship. It's their atheists' cathedral. Father no doubt designed it with deity in mind. His own. The building blocks are hewn from limestone, the ceilings high and the windows cliff-like, flooding the whole structure with light. There's even a slanted window strategically placed in the conference hall, which channels a shaft of light directly at the podium when the sun is in the right spot – late morning. The AGM is scheduled for 11am. You have to hand it to him, I suppose; he knows how to work a crowd.

I pick at a muffin – apple and cinnamon with a crunchy crumble topping – and wait for the bell to ring. I intentionally avoid eye contact with the other attendees. The last thing I feel like is making small talk. There's a guy on the other side of the room who keeps glancing over at me. I hope to God he doesn't approach. I turn away and pretend to listen to the string quartet in the corner, declining a glass of champagne from a passing waiter. A ball of anger starts to form in the pit of my stomach. Anger at the extravagance. The waste. For Father to claim that there were insufficient funds for vaccine research and then to lavish money on an event like this is absurd.

When the bell finally sounds at 10:50am, I head into the conference hall and towards the stage. An automaton, ready to take my place at the end of the row of M.A.D.E. Directors' chairs. Not to say anything, of course. My role is ceremonial at best. Just to be seen. I don't bother to smile.

I remember going to meetings like this as a young boy. Seeing Father on stage speaking about this plan he had. A plan to cheat death. To cheat the bacteria that he saw as our ultimate enemy. The building was different back then – far smaller, and there were only a handful of shareholders present, a core group of moneyed disciples who didn't laugh at his ideas but instead gazed in awe at him, seeing him as the prophet that I suppose in many ways he was. His presence, his force of will, seemed to dwarf everything and everyone else in the room. He seemed like a god to me then. A guardian angel. Blood blinds. I think he was exactly the same man then as he is now. People say that power corrupts, but I'm not altogether sure that's correct. It may well be closer to the truth to say that only the truly corrupted, the sociopaths who walk amongst us, only they are capable of achieving absolute power. Only they are prepared to seize it, whatever the moral cost.

Five minutes pass, giving everyone enough time to find and take their seats and to allow just the right level of excitement to spark and hum. *Timing is everything. Start too soon, your audience isn't focused; stall too long and you've lost them.* My father. Ever the showman.

The main lights dim and he leaps onto the stage. The whole back wall has been turned into a screen of swirling neon green neurons, light pulsing along them, a brain firing. A sudden music shift and next up is a single purple-stained bacterium, which starts to divide by binary fission until, within seconds, purple bacteria have covered the whole screen. The music shifts again and then there are faces – all races, all ages – one morphing into the next into the next into the next. The effect is dizzying. Just as you are approaching sensory overload, the images slow down, coalesce and then tumble down into five words:

We Are M.A.D.E. of Memories.

The first and last two words fade until only the initials M.A.D.E. are left. Finally, the letters move apart and the full company name: MEMORY AND DATA EVOLUTION fills the space. The Ltd is much smaller.

Father lets them hang there for a count of three and then begins, his rich baritone filling the hall. I've heard the speech dozens of times before, as has nearly everyone in the room. Only very few people a year manage to earn and save enough to upgrade to a Level One insurance policy; the yearly fees are astronomical. And, even then, you might not qualify. You have to be the 'right sort' of person. I doubt there are more than a handful of new recruits here. But no one seems to mind the repetition. On occasion, I've even spotted a couple mouthing along in the semi-dark; the speech a comforting catechism, a shared history, which explains their place in the world, and how and why they belong.

'It all began thirty-six years ago in a hospital room not a hundred metres from this spot. My mother, only fifty-two at the time, was dying from what we would later identify as Staph. Half her life left unlived. Cast your minds back, those of you who can remember that time…

'There had been short-lived viral pandemics, incidents that seemed world-altering at the time but in hindsight were nothing. Death from infection was still a relative rarity. Amputees unusual. People went to hospital to recover not to die. A course of antibiotics should have been all it took to destroy the bacteria that had taken root in my mother's body and restore her to full health.

'But the antibiotics had no effect on her. Nor on the forty-five million other mothers and fathers and sons and daughters who died that year. The government had negligently allowed the overuse of antibiotics, stripping them of their utility and allowing an array of resistant microbes to develop. They completely underestimated the impact of horizontal gene transfer that enabled antibiotic resistance to pass between bacterial species. Their focus was elsewhere: The economy. Global warming. Curbing the reach of corporations.' *Bark laugh*. 'As if that was where the danger lay.

'As I held my mother dying in my arms, I had a moment of absolute clarity. An epiphany. If the government cannot protect us, then we must change the government. If the body cannot outlive bacteria, then we must outlive the body...'

The hall bursts into rapturous applause and I start to zone out. It's the hospital bit that gets me every time. The picture he paints of the grieving son. Lies. All lies. Not Granny being ill. It was before I was born, but Mother told me that was true enough. The circumstances were different though, she said. Granny didn't die in his arms. In reality she was on a dirty, overcrowded ward. Mother held her hand, mottled blue, as blood-flecked coughs racked her body. Father was in a meeting.

It's almost funny, in a way, that it is tiny microscopic cells that have decimated us as a species. Everyone thought it would be global warming. When years of European and Chinese-led initiatives brought net carbon emissions to zero by 2050 we all breathed a collective and smug sigh of relief. The arrogance of humans to think we know everything. The illusion of control.

My focus returns to the podium. To Father.

'In time, people recognised the importance of my work into longevity. They appreciated that the solution to this emergency lay in the minds of the leading scientists and investors and that these minds must not be allowed to perish. That they must continue to process and calculate and *solve*. The less educated scoffed. Yes, it's *true*, they scoffed at our proposals. They thought we were talking about brain transplants. "Brain transplants won't work," they cried. "The brain tissue will be rejected. The brain cells will still age and decay." But they didn't understand. They lacked vision. The mind is separate from the body. It transcends the body. Descartes realised this around four hundred years ago; although he lacked our scientific insight. He talked in terms of the soul. But the mind doesn't reside in cells or in tissue, but rather in electrical impulses. The brain itself is nothing more than a

33

biological computer – a data processor. And what are memories but stored electrical data? Data which can be transferred, intact and uncorrupted, into another biological computer.'

Father stretches and clicks his neck to the right. It's where he stores tension. It's been the same in every body he's possessed. He starts to talk about the mechanism of transition, the uploading and downloading of data and then segues into the selection process: '... so that you can be guaranteed that you are transitioning into a Host whose brain is fully functioning and equally adept at storing, accessing and processing your thoughts and memories.'

A hand rises four rows from the front on the right. I don't recognise the face but that doesn't mean she's new. She could just have transitioned since last year. I doubt it, though. Anyone who's been around for a while would know how Father feels about interruptions.

Father ignores the hand and keeps talking.

The hand stays up.

He continues to ignore her.

'Excuse me?' she calls out. That settles it. She's definitely new.

Father clicks his neck to the left. 'Yes?' His voice has a sharpened edge.

'Did you consider transitioning into robots?'

'Did – I – consider – transitioning – into – robots...?'

Father drags each word out and wears the sort of patronising smile you'd save for watching an infant roll around in its own excrement. 'Let me ask you something…?'

'Janet.'

'Let me ask you something, *Janet*. Would you like to be a robot?'

'Um … no, I guess not.'

Father raises both hands in a magician's shrug and the audience titters appreciatively.

But the hand is up again. This is definitely her first AGM. And probably her last.

'What about clones? Did you consider clones?'

'So … many … questions. Yes, the scientists at the *forefront* of technological invention did consider clones, but after detailed psychological research we ruled them out. You see, Janet, we are talking about immortality. People do not want to look the same forever. To have their partner look the same forever. They want variety. They need variety to stop them from blowing their brains out after eighty years. And what if the cloning process goes wrong? If you had to dispose of body after body of your Original at various stages of development? Or the psychological impact of seeing ten different 'you's in storage. It simply wouldn't work. Instead, Hosts are generated randomly using donated eggs and sperm from all Level Ones, grown in Womb Pods and then developed in Centres. They are generally attractive, physically gifted, with high brain-capacity. The bodies belong to all of us. They are all of us…'

The screen bursts into life again:

We Are In This Together.

Having successfully turned the conversation round to his next sound bite, Father clicks his neck one final time and then steamrollers to the end of his presentation.

As soon as the lights are up, I follow him off the stage. The vein pulsing in his neck tells to me stay clear, but I ignore it, worried about what hellfire he's about to unleash on that woman. He ignores me, instead grabbing the arm of the Head of Security who's standing in the wings, earpiece in.

'She never comes in here again,' Father hisses. 'Downgrade her.'

'You can't do that,' I interject and then curse myself. The worst possible thing to do when Father is riled like this is to tell him what he can and can't do.

He swivels in my direction and I receive the full force of his rage.

'When you've set up a multibillion-pound company from scratch, maybe I'll listen to your opinions. But for now, shut up.'

Father's outburst has given Doug Henshaw, Head of Legal, time to finish crossing the hall and join us. His face is red and sweaty, the twenty metre half-jog having destroyed him. No wonder he transitions so frequently, he takes no care of his bodies at all.

'Michael, [*gasp for air*] Arthur's right. We can't downgrade people. Not unless they fail to keep up with their scheduled payments. It's in the contract.'

'Damn the contract. I won't have her in here again, shooting her ignorant mouth off. How did this even happen? Wasn't she screened?'

Doug tries again, hunching his shoulders, bending his knees; the physical manifestation of grovelling reverence. The beta to Father's alpha. He's a good man, deep down. And he knows how to handle Father.

'She was screened. She passed all of our background checks. She's Janet Hurst – the head of Terrafirm. They're very influential. It might not be wise to make an enemy of her.'

That explained it. How she'd managed to build up enough wealth to buy in. Terrafirm were the closest to settling Mars. While Father had been working out how to outlive bacteria, others had been working out how to leave them behind. New planet. New microbial spectrum. A chance to start again.

'Well, put her at the bottom of the list for transition. She no longer chooses. If there's a body with a limp or a squint or a two-digit IQ, don't dispose of it. She gets it instead.'

'But the contract…'

'Get it done.'

I leave the building in a haze, so I hardly register the protestor at the bottom of the stone steps. It's only the egg that lands and breaks on my forehead that fully alerts me to his presence. Golden yolk descends my face; albumen clinging to my eyebrows and lashes.

'Murderer,' he shouts, staring directly at me. '*Murderer.*'

The filter mask he and all the DMWs wear covers the lower half of his face so all I can see is his eyes. And they burn with hate.

A security guard leaps into action and drags the man away, but I'm still left shaken.

A stranger. A complete stranger hates me. Not just my father. But me.

I head home, walking quickly, sticking to the main roads, but I can't shed the prickles of fear. And I can't shake the feeling that someone is following me.

ALBA

I wake, exhausted, having hardly slept, thoughts of Curly chasing round my head. The dorm is too hot and my back and forehead are damp from sweat. The wind had changed direction yesterday evening and was coming from the Wilderness. When this happens the Guardians always shut all the windows to limit the radiation. Lying in bed in the dark, I could still smell it though, sweet and putrid, and I imagined it seeping into the bricks and glass, contaminating us all.

The bell for Morning Meeting rings and I file into the hall, sandwiched between F3106 and F3114: Freckles and Bluey. I like them. They're my friends, but they don't know me. Really know me like Curly did. Bluey tugs at my sleeve as we sit down.

'What is it?'

'Your hair.' I reach up to touch it and my hand meets a wiry bird's nest. Damn. I forgot to brush it again. I can't even have looked in the mirror or I'd have noticed. I always had Curly to remind me about things like this. I'll have to make sure none of the Guardians notice. The Creator's Fourth Commandment: *A smart appearance reflects a smart mind.*

'Here.' Bluey removes a spare hair band from her wrist and passes it to me and I quickly improvise a bun.

Just in time, as a second later the Supervisor is on stage, scanning the faces lined up before her.

She is in a foul mood – her mouth the thinnest straight line and a muscle leaping in her right cheek. I thank the Creator that Bluey had a spare band.

'One of you has been seen washing their hands once rather than the required three times when coming inside after Games,' she barked.

We all slouch lower, trying to distance ourselves from her searchlight eyes. Could it be me? I feel the panic rise and the flutter in my chest. I always try to remember the required three – *for Home, for the Creator, for Myself* – but there's always a chance I'd forgotten.

'M3009, approach the stage.'

The rest of us breathe a sigh of relief as the culprit drags himself forward, head slung low. I don't know him. We don't have much contact with the boys. Their dorms are on the other side of the building and they're taught separately in accordance with the Creator's Fifth Commandment.

The Supervisor draws back her hand and slaps M3009 once, hard, across the face. His lip splits crimson.

We all gasp. It'll leave a mark. Visible for at least a few days. You'd see it in the next video for sure.

'Never forget,' the Supervisor continues, her voice clipped. 'Cleanliness is next to Godliness.'

'Praise the Creator,' we all intone, as M3009 returns to the herd, red-eyed.

She pulls out a handkerchief and wipes her hands as if they've been sullied, but says nothing as a screen descends behind her. Only when it shudders to a halt, fully extended, does she next speak.

'This is the latest News Bulletin from the Research City. Pay attention, please.'

With that, she stands to the side and clicks 'play'.

The camera sweeps through the Wilderness. Blackened heather, scrub bushes, short brown grass. No animals. No people. The land will be contaminated for another hundred or so years unless the Research City scientists discover a faster way to cleanse it. The camera changes direction and three scientists come into shot. They are dressed in big, white hazmat suits with clear visors that you can see their faces through. Faces furrowed in concentration at the magnitude of the task facing them. I zone out of the accompanying voiceover and instead stare at the faces, one at a time. These are the people risking it all to keep us safe. Our heroes. I need to stop my ingratitude. My selfishness. I need to focus so that I can do my part. So that I can join them.

My eyes rest on the third face, the one at the back and

my heart triple jumps. It's Curly! It has to be! Dark curls, pinned to the side of her face by the helmet. Perfectly spaced eyes. Rosebud lips. Dimples ... wait ... no! NO! Cheek dimples only. No third dimple. No Bermuda triangle. Someone else. Someone else entirely. I don't know why the realisation crushes me so completely. It's not like anything would have changed if it had been her. I couldn't have spoken to her through the screen or anything. I just wish she'd write soon. I know she'll be busy settling in and everything. That cleansing the Wilderness takes priority. But she promised. She promised me.

The film ends and we offer up the prayer of thanks.

Thank you, Creator, for keeping us safe.

Thank you, Creator, for feeding us.

Thank you, Creator, for teaching us so that we do not repeat humanity's mistakes.

Thank you, Creator. We praise you.

I think of the poor souls left out in the Wilderness. Mutated and dying. It reminds me how lucky I am to be here and how important the work of the Research City is. How I must improve myself so that I am worthy to join them.

ARTHUR

One of Tommy's hands is dangling off the side of the punt, the other cradles a bottle of Champagne. Only the navy smudges under his eyes belie the picture of decadent loucheness he's always so keen to project.

I've got the pole and I'm doing my best to navigate us free from a patch of river weed and the half-submerged log to our right. I use the log for purchase, push off and nearly topple in. There's no doubt about it – my balance is getting worse.

'Here. Let's stop here,' Tommy drawls a few minutes later. 'Perfect spot for a picnic.' I acquiesce, mooring the punt to the trunk of a nearby weeping willow. Its leaves are golden and beginning to shed. *Fall, leaves, fall; die, flowers, away.*

We're not far from the banks of Christchurch, Father's old college. I'd been expected to go there too. Before. When people still thought it was a good idea to live communally. To share bathrooms. To eat side by side in halls. The building is now empty, of course; lessons all online. They haven't demolished it though and it still stands there, silent and alone – a monument to the dead

– or an artefact waiting. For the resurgence of humanity. Maybe if Parachute increase their efforts. If other laboratories join them. If I can finally wring the funding out of Father. Maybe we'll find the vaccines we need to make this a reality.

We climb out the punt and lay a rug on the ground. Further up the grass there's a cluster of other picnickers. All Level Ones. The lack of masks is the obvious giveaway, but it's more than that. It's the casual way in which their bodies are splayed across the grass, the braying laughter that ambles in our direction, the casual celebration of an unexpected Indian Summer. Tommy inclines his head in their direction, suggesting that we join them, but I shake mine in reply. I'm not in the mood for a group. For forced joviality.

Slightly further up on the grass sits a man by himself. I can't shake the feeling that he's staring at me.

'So, Arthur, old chap. Why no change? I'm bored of your face. Go get a new one.'

Tommy is one of the few people I've told about the tumour and I know this is Tommy-speak for *transition quickly, I'm worried about you*, but it still grates. Everything has to be a joke with him. Or at least couched as one.

'I'll organise it soon.'

'Do that,' says Tommy, suddenly serious, his mood typically mercurial. 'Or your father will choose for you, and God knows who you'll wake up as.'

He's right. I know he's right. As if by way of confirmation, my phone vibrates again in my pocket, reminding me of the message I've been ignoring. It's from M.A.D.E.'s in-house psychologist; I recognise the number. I haven't listened to it yet, choosing instead to dig the phone deep into the pockets of my cords; burying the red flashing light. It'll be reminding me to book my pre-transition appointment. Psychological assessment pre-transition is mandatory, but I can still sense Father's hand in the background, pulling the strings.

I take a bite out of a smoked salmon sandwich and lie back on the grass, cloud watching.

Boat.

Swan.

House.

Atom cloud.

The naming calms me.

'So, what's happening with Karen?' Tommy interrupts my thoughts with a grin. 'You haven't brought her out for ages. Daisy's been asking after her.'

'It didn't work out,' I reply shortly. I don't want to think about Karen. I want to look at the clouds.

'She's a good-looking girl.'

'I know,' I snap back. Karen's beautiful. At least, her current incarnation is. Long, tawny hair, blue eyes, a perfect button nose. 'But she doesn't do anything.'

45

Tommy lets out a throaty chuckle. 'Then you should date Ellen. She does *everything*.'

The clouds are just clouds again and I sit up. Normally I would have laughed along, but today his words taste metallic.

'That's not what I mean and you know it.' I'm angry now and Tommy's annoying me. His too-long fringe. His laconic expression. The way he rests his head on his hand, tilted at a perfect forty-five-degree angle.

'Sorry. I was just trying to cheer you up. To distract you.' Tommy's tone is sincere, the drawl banished, and I begin to forgive him. I can never stay angry at him for long. I remember the navy smudges. For all his bravado, Tommy is troubled. He rarely sleeps and relies on a system of uppers and downers to survive the day.

'Seriously, start looking tonight, Arthur,' he continues. 'I'll come over and we'll go through the brochure together. The doctor talked about potential memory loss if you didn't transition quickly, didn't he? I wouldn't want to lose any of my best friend. Even if his mind is annoyingly prudish and judgmental.'

The drawl is back and finally I join in the laughter.

'And we do need to get you laid again,' Tommy continues. 'I know there's no girl that's ever worthy enough for you, but maybe, for once, view it not as a meeting of minds, but something physical, purely physical.

Say, if you had to choose one of those fine fillies ahead…
No, I know you don't *know* them,' he adds, pre-empting
my objections, 'but say you had to choose one purely on
looks – play my game this once – come on, pretty please,
who would you go for?'

'Um… You know I hate this.'

'Humour me. Don't think – choose.'

'OK. OK. Well … the one with the long brown hair.'

'Final decision?'

'Yes. Why?

Tommy collapses in a hysterical heap. It's several
minutes before he regains the power of speech.

'What? Come on, Tommy.' The irritation is starting to
return.

'It's … just … that…' Tommy manages to get out in
between bouts of breathlessness, 'that's Davina.'

I mime incomprehension. I can't remember meeting a
Davina.

'Last week she was Dave. You *hated* Dave.'

I throw the rest of my sandwich in Tommy's face, but
he's still laughing.

'It's not my fault you missed her New Body Party. Don't
look so surprised, Arthur. My, you're uptight. It's 2084;
gender's fluid. Why spend eternity confined to one sex? I
fully intend to experiment. Oh, but your face. Ha! Your
face! You are your father's son after all.'

ALBA

The air smells like wet grass, last night's rain somehow trapping and magnifying the smell. I like it. I always have. I think I prefer outdoors to indoors. Helping with the animals and tending the vegetables rather than studying. Watching the morning mist roll away, I think how amazing it must have been before there was the Wilderness. When you could go anywhere. When your limits were cliffs and oceans and mountain ranges rather than concrete walls.

The rota has me down for barn duty so I go to the shed and pull on waterproofs – trousers, jacket and wellies until I'm covered in 360 degrees of plastic. There's no mirror but I can tell I look ridiculous. Like I'm in a really low-budget hazmat suit minus the face guard.

Roly – that's what Curly and I named Pig 11 – is lying outstretched on his straw bed. He's only coming up to six months old, but you'd never have guessed it from his size. He's enormous. Like he's swallowed about three other pigs and is now lying down happily to digest them. At the other end of the barn in a separate pen, the younger piglets are with the sow, snorting and snuffling around their food trough, guzzling up the leftover porridge and scraps. The boar's kept in a separate barn along with the cows.

I ignore the little ones. Roly's my favourite. I scratch him behind his ears and he grunts. It's his soft spot. There and behind his right shoulder. We're not supposed to touch the animals, but I always wash my hands the requisite three times afterwards so I don't see what harm it can do.

I notice that Roly's food trough is still empty so I take the bucket from the corner and go to fill it up from the big yellow bin near the side door where any food scraps, vegetable peelings and so on go. Halfway there, Guardian 8 blocks my path, eyes squinting through his blond fringe.

'No need for that,' he says gruffly, nodding at the bucket. His arms are awkwardly positioned. He's holding something behind his back. I can't tell what.

'But his trough's empty,' I reply. 'He hasn't been fed yet this morning.'

'He won't be needing it,' Guardian 8 says. 'It's his time.'

My heart sinks. I know why we rear pigs. We need the meat and it's too dangerous to bring it in from outside as it might be poisoned by the radiation. But it still gets me every time.

He brings his arms forward, revealing a rifle.

'Go fetch Guardians 4 and 11,' he instructs. 'We won't be able to hang the body without a bit more help.'

I do as instructed and then follow the Guardians to the barn, dragging my feet as I walk to try and slow everything down. To stop time.

'F3527!' Guardian 8 calls. 'Hurry up. I need you to keep it calm.'

Reluctantly, I climb into the pen. Roly's standing now, snout lowered, rooting around in the trough, impatient for his promised breakfast. I stand next to him, scratching the top of his head again.

'You'll have to move your hand.'

I switch position and scratch behind his right shoulder instead.

Roly looks up and spots the gun which Guardian 8 is now raising, aiming for the spot just above the centre of his eyes. A flash of understanding passes across Roly's face. I swear it does. People think pigs are stupid, but they're not. The look isn't one of fear, really. More like surprise mixed with indignation. Anger at the realisation that the life he thought he was going to lead was now going to be over so abruptly. That he wasn't being sheltered and cared for and fed because we loved him but because we had a use for him. His whole reality was crumbling. And all I could do was stand there, scratching his shoulder, in a pathetic attempt to ease his passing.

I couldn't help hang him afterwards. He was too heavy for me to be of any use so the other Guardians elbowed me out of the way. I'm pleased though. I didn't want to see his neck cut, to see the straw turn red.

Later they'll cut up the body and freeze all the meat. Then at night they burn the remains of the carcass so as not to attract rats. The air fills with a rancid sweetness that reminds me of the smell when the winds come from the Wilderness. It makes a kind of sense that radiation and death smell the same.

ARTHUR

I'm hurrying into the building so I don't hear the doorman the first time. I'm vaguely aware that he's speaking but I don't make out the words.

He clears his throat and tries again.

'Sir. Mr Easton, sir. There's a message for you.'

'Yes?' My manner is curter than it needs to be and I immediately regret its tone. After all, the man's just doing his job.

'You're to call a Dr Saunders. At your earliest convenience. He was most insistent, sir.'

I smile inwardly. They never give up, these people. I don't return their voicemails so they track me down to my apartment. I'll have to schedule that appointment just to get them off my back.

It's only then that I realise that something's off. I turn to look more closely at the man I'm talking to and realise that it's not my normal doorman I'm addressing. It's the same uniform – the deep velvet burgundy with the gold trim – but whereas Larry is tall, lanky with fair hair scraped back from his brow, the man in front of me is shorter, wider and with darker hair and sunken, watchful eyes.

'Where's Larry?' I ask, confused.

The man's hesitation and quick downwards glance tells me everything I need to know. Not another one. Poor fellow. Poor, poor fellow.

'What took him?' I ask, hoping my interest does not come across as morbid curiosity. It isn't. Larry had been here six years. A good man and a constant in my life. I genuinely wish to understand.

'Staph,' the new man replies. His body seems to tense as he says it. An involuntary response to the modern Reaper. Then he gives himself a barely perceptible shake as if pulling himself together.

'I'm Charles, sir. I'll be taking over all of his duties. Rest assured it will be a seamless transition.'

'That was not my concern,' I say tersely. I don't know why I feel the need to justify myself, but I do. I don't want this new man to think I am completely heartless.

'I should send the family something,' I say. The 'should' sounds wrong. 'I want to send the family something.'

'A mini-muffin basket, perhaps?' Charles' delivery is faultlessly polite but I can't shake the feeling that he's mocking me.

'No. No, that's not what I had in mind at all.' I take out my wallet and unfold it. From the central compartment I remove a thick pile of notes and, hands shaking, I quickly count them. Six hundreds, seven fifties and five twenties. It's not much but it'll keep them going for a while. I roll them up and press them towards Charles.

'Please make sure this reaches Larry's widow.' I think for a moment. 'He does have a widow, doesn't he?'

'Yes, there's a widow, sir.'

It strikes me how little I know about Larry's life. About the lives of any of the people who inhabit the periphery of my existence.

I walk towards the lift, my mood sombre. Doorman to a prestigious apartment block like this is a well-paid job but also a dangerous one. There are only Level Ones in the building and hygiene levels are high, but still the number of germs one must be exposed to through daily contact with over twenty residents... I glance back at Charles and it suddenly strikes me – he's standing there, as Larry did – face exposed, hands bare. Taking completely unnecessary risks for a Level Two.

'Charles,' I ask, 'why don't you wear a face mask, or gloves even? Might that not be a sensible precaution?'

A smirk rises to the surface of his face and then submerges again so quickly I begin to doubt it were ever present at all.

'They're not permitted, sir – company policy. Residents like to see people's faces. It puts them at ease.'

'Which company?' I ask, my ire beginning to build. I couldn't alter the fact of Larry's death but I could make it mean something by bringing the company to account. Changing the rules for future employees.

'Your company, sir. They own this apartment block. And most of the … premier … blocks in town.'

'Right,' I say, feeling like a bloody fool. I know so little about the workings of the organisation I'm supposedly on the board of. Acting like a gallant knight riding to save the villagers when my family actually supplied the dragon.

'Will that be all, sir?'

'Yes. Thank you, Charles,' I say. Again, it's only subtle but there's something about the way he looks at me. An echo of the protestor's eyes. Diluted hate.

I head towards the lift, and a movement outside on the street pulls my eye. I stare out through the lobby's huge mock-Georgian windows. There's a face looking in. At me. But before I can properly focus on it, it's gone.

ALBA

It's Wednesday and I'm awake before the sun. I'm not normally a morning person but today I'm buzzing. There are no remains-of-sleep-fog to find my way out of. I probably burnt through that at around five. Today is 'Physical and Interview morning' and I'm ready. This is my new approach – I decided upon it last night in a flash of genius – *stop moping and look forward to and make the most of every opportunity to shine in front of the Mentors.* This way I'll get chosen quicker and be back with Curly again.

After breakfast I'm first in to see the doctor.

'Good morning, Doctor,' I smile in a hopefully engaging and chirpy manner.

His mouth remains a straight line. He's not really one for niceties.

'Sit here,' he points to the end of the long, padded table he has in his office. 'Knees a little way off the edge – yes, like that. Can you swing them freely?'

'Yes, Doctor.' The chirp is still there.

'Right.'

He holds up his hand and then raps it sharply just below

my knee cap. My lower leg kicks forward involuntarily and Dr Jones makes a mark on his clipboard. So far, so good, I smile to myself. When M2989 failed his knee jerk test last Physical he got transferred to a different Home to recuperate and while that might sound really nice and relaxing, I don't have time for that at the moment. I've got a Mentor to win.

Next up, eyes. I have to stare at this bright light while he checks that my pupils constrict and dilate properly and then stare at a screen whilst wearing an eye patch and press a button every time I see a tiny flash of green light. Then I have to try and keep my eye open while he puffs air into it to check for something – glaucoma, I think. I blink at the first two attempts and Dr Jones makes a spluttering noise of exasperation. It's hard though. Really hard. Surely blinking if a huge puff of air is hurtling towards your eyeball is a sign of a healthily functioning eye? For all the eye knows, the air might be a giant diseased fly about to land. I manage to keep both eyes open on the third attempt and give myself an imaginary pat on the back.

Eye tests are followed by checks of my heart rate and blood pressure and I can relax for these as I can't mess them up. It's just a question of staying still as a band inflates and then deflates around my upper arm and then keeping calm while a sensor is wrapped round my finger with a Velcro strip.

The blood tests are trickier. I hate the sight of blood.

Always have. I turn away as the vials fill with a deep maroon and are labelled before being sent away to test for inflammation markers, rheumatoid factor and a host of other random diseases. I think they test different stuff every month. I wonder what it'll be this time. My mouth opens to ask, but then I hear Curly's voice in my head – *don't ask so many questions, they don't like questions,* so I close it again and bite my lip to keep it shut.

'Urine.'

I reach down to the bag by my feet and pull out the sample pot. It's still warm. Dr Jones opens the lid, failing to disguise the distaste he feels, and I blush pink while he dips the long piece of analytical paper in and compares the colours it turns to the chart on the wall.

'Undress and lie down flat on the table.' Again, it's an instruction rather than a request, but I don't let it dampen my mood and I do as he asks, putting my clothes in a neat pile on the chair. His hands are cold. Touching my neck, stomach, inside thigh. Feeling. Prodding. He keeps his fingers on my breasts for the longest and I hold my breath, worrying that he's found something, but his expression doesn't change and finally he lifts them and brushes his hands against his coat as if to wipe them clean.

'No sign of raised glands, cysts or other abnormalities,' he says, ticking another box. He's not talking to me. He's not looking at me. It's more like he's talking to the clipboard as he writes. Passing time. 'Query raised mole on right shoulder. Unaesthetic, but no signs of discolouration.'

His eyes land on me again and he frowns.

'You may dress yourself. Send F3614 in next.'

ARTHUR

'Arthur! Welcome, welcome… It's been a while.'

'Two years, three months.'

'Two years? Is that all? Staph infection?'

'No, brain tumour.'

'I see… Unusual.'

I feel rattled already, even though I know Dr Saunders hasn't objectively said anything wrong. It's his tone. Manufactured warmth with side notes of smugness. A tone reserved for children with whom one only pretends to engage. A teacher who's chosen to teach primary out of a desire for superiority rather than a love of young minds. I half expect him to comment on how much I've grown. I hate the man. I should have ignored the message for longer. This is all Tommy's fault. He said he wouldn't help me select until I'd been. That my apprehension was simply mild paranoia brought on by the tumour. I shouldn't have told him that I think someone's following me.

Dr Saunders gestures towards a chair in the corner. It's made from aged dark brown leather and is slightly reclined. Not a couch, but near enough. I walk over and sit down. All my muscles tense as I stare up at the ceiling, wondering where the bug is. In the corner underneath the ornate cornicing? Or maybe not in the ceiling at all. Maybe in the standard lamp? Or concealed under the desk?

Dr Saunders dims the lights and slows his voice. My muscles twist and knot.

'This is *your* time, Arthur. Your chance to discuss any concerns you may have over the upcoming transitioning process. I am here to facilitate this process. Not to judge. Everything you say will be treated with the utmost discretion.'

Liar. Big. Fat. Liar. Dr Saunders isn't projecting his voice, so the bug must be close to him. Under the desk or possibly in the paperweight on top. A purple-stained jellyfish suspended in glass with a suspiciously thick base. No one uses paperweights any more. I wonder if Father is listening to this now or recording it for later consumption. Over a cigar or two.

'Are you experiencing any feelings of paranoia?'

'No,' I reply flatly. I don't tell him about the people following me on the street. About the face in the window. It would just mean more brain scans. And they'd force me to transition sooner.

I don't say anything else and Dr Saunders also remains silent, hoping to coax me into spilling my guts into the vacuum. I continue to stare at the ceiling. He caves first.

'Do you have any fears about the transition process?'

'No,' I reply curtly.

'Why do you think you've been delaying coming to see me?'

'I've been busy.'

'I see.' His words suspend and then drift.

I still give him nothing so he changes tack. Starts supplying the information himself.

'I imagine transitioning must bring up difficult memories of your mother…' (*Leave Mother out of this*, I want to hiss.) '…Of your first transition.'

Shut up! Shut up! I scream inside. And then I think: why am I keeping this in? Father's listening, so let him hear this. Let him suffer.

'Mother wasn't like other women. Other people,' I begin. I know that, if I looked up, I'd see a superior smile spread over Dr Saunders' lips – he's cracked me, manipulated me into talking – but I force myself to continue. Father will hear this. If there's any humanity left in him, he will hear this and bleed.

'She was clever and funny. Sharp and kind. She had this air of untouchable glamour, but then she'd let out a raucous, dirty laugh and catch you completely off-guard.'

'She was a very emotional lady,' Dr Saunders interrupts, his voice beginning to sound wary, already regretting bringing Mother up, already trying to paint her as unstable, as damaged.

'No, I wouldn't say that,' I reply, levelly, my tone an

implicit reprimand. 'She had depth, that's all. And her eyes. Lots of people have dead eyes. Fish eyes. They look at you, and the world around them, but they don't *see*. Mother's eyes were clear blue and they saw everything. If she looked at you – at me,' I can feel my throat constricting, my tear ducts filling – 'she saw all the way through the outside, the superficial, peeling through layer after layer until she saw your soul.'

'Yes, she was a very religious lady.' He's doing it again. Twisting my words. Anger dams the tears.

'She had faith, like many people. She wasn't a member of a cult.'

'That's not what I was implying.'

I ignore him and continue. This is *my* time, after all.

'When we came down with the infection – her, my friend Tommy, and I – she knew she was going to die; that all three of us were, and she didn't want to come back. She was very clear about it and although the fever was ravaging her body, her mental faculties were still intact. *Sound of mind*, you'd call it. Father was the only one who wasn't ill. She told him explicitly that she'd had her time on Earth and had made her peace with her passing. She even recorded video clips to say goodbye. Father didn't listen, of course. Said he needed her continued support. Thought it'd be bad for business if his own wife 'refused the treatment'. So he brought her back.'

63

'I'm sure you're not remembering this exactly as it happened. The mind can play tricks on one. False memory syndrome is quite common when a child is faced with a parental suicide, particularly when it's maternal. The loss of a mother is a traumatic episode. The child invents external causes when the real trigger is internal – in her case, depression. It is quite understandable and your tumour will be exacerbating these feelings of confusion.' Dr Saunders' voice is raised now, and faster. There's an almost pleading edge to it. He needs me to agree. To admit to delusions. He's imagining the repercussions he'll suffer from Father. I block him out.

'He brought her back. It was 2059 and he brought her back in the body of a blonde, twenty-three-year-old with huge tits and no waist. Bastard. Bastard. Bastard. Her eyes were no longer clear. They were covered in the same fog as everyone else's. She wasn't unstable. She wasn't a religious nut. She was never depressed before. She killed herself because she couldn't handle being in a new body. Couldn't handle that her son looked different. Couldn't handle that her husband was the same.'

I give up trying to hold it together and I'm sobbing now. Coughing and crying and shaking on the chair. I look up and for the first time Dr Saunders is staring at me with something resembling compassion.

He says nothing as I leave the room.

64

ALBA

I spend the rest of the morning preparing for the interview, knowing how all-important it is. I've figured if you're a Mentor and you want to know who to choose as an Apprentice, you'd definitely want someone clever who did well in exams, but more important even than that, you'd want someone sparky. Someone who could make creative leaps in their research and who would really push towards new discoveries. Someone you'd want to spend every day with.

At 11:50am I enter Interview Room 2. It's more like a big cupboard than a room. The walls are white to bounce the light onto our faces and padded to help with soundproofing. There's a wall-mounted camera on the back left-hand corner and then a small desk in the other corner with a computer monitor and a keyboard with various switches and dials where the technician sits. I sit in the swivel chair in the centre and rotate it left. The camera is pointed straight at me, the lights bright in my face. Instinctively I feel my spine bend inwards; a protective curling up. I hear Curly's voice in my head. *Sit up straight. No hunching. Look the camera in the eye. No one would like to work with a weird, shifty, side-gazer. Sound knowledgeable, but willing to learn; confident but not arrogant.*

'Ready?' the technician drones in a nasally voice. He's clearly less than thrilled to be here.

'Yes.'

The red light at the top of the camera turns on.

The interview begins as always with the same basic questions. Prompts for information, really. They're all pre-recorded so it's not even the technician speaking (luckily this time as they might associate his horrific voice with mine and lower my chances.) The technicians are just there to make sure the recording works and to upload it afterwards.

'State your age,' says the disembodied, super-calm female voice.

'Seventeen,' I say confidently into the camera, forcing my eyes to stay level. Imaginary Mentor, I am looking you straight in the eye. What are you going to do about it? Pick me, that's what.

'State your height.'

'165cm.'

'State your weight.'

'51kg.'

'And your other key measurements.'

'34cm, 28cm, 36cm.'

'State your Averaged Test Score.'

'91.'

There's nothing I can do here to impress. To make myself memorable. And they get all these results anyway so it's not like I can lie.

Next comes some mental maths – *324 times 6.450 divided by 15*. I like maths so it's not too taxing. I focus on trying to stop my forehead weirdly wrinkling up and my bottom lip sagging as I calculate. A few science questions follow. *How would you manufacture Bromoethane? Describe the wave and particle nature of light.* And then a bit of recall. *Recite a passage of your choosing.*

This week I've chosen to read a poem – *The Brook* by Tennyson. I came across an old, battered poetry anthology in the library and I couldn't put it down. I liked all the poems but this one is by far my favourite. I don't know why I like it so much. I've never even seen a brook apart from on a screen. Or a river for that matter. But I can imagine it. Vividly. I looked up every description from the poem in a nature encyclopaedia. The forget-me-nots and skimming swallows and golden gravel. It's how I imagine the world will be when the Research City scientists finally cleanse the Wilderness. Nature, ready to re-emerge from its cocoon, beautiful and unsullied.

For men may come and men may go, but I go on forever.
Hopefully it will speak to the Mentors too.

'Now please deliver your Personal Statement.'

I take a deep breath. This is it. Five minutes to talk about any issue of my choosing. My chance to shine. I've given this lots of thought. Most people, me included, usually talk about their interests or achievements – a new fitness personal best, something we've made in art, an interesting fact we've covered this week in lessons. But would these things really interest a Mentor? I don't think so. I've been working out how to prove my worth and been thinking about everything they show the scientists doing in the updates we get in Morning Meetings. We always see scientists in a lab testing soil samples or scientists out in hazmat suits on burnt, blackened ground. But the land I can see beyond the walls, stretching far, far to the horizon isn't blackened. The start of the Wilderness is still green and looks pretty similar to Safety so maybe we should focus on this first? Make this habitable before we concentrate on the blackened stuff?

And I've been thinking that rather than just soil, we could also focus on animals as markers of radiation levels. Not that any come near here, of course. The Supervisor makes sure of it. If they're from the Wilderness, they'd make us sick. That's why we have spikes on the roofs and walls to stop birds landing and dogs to chase them away if they do. But I've seen birds in the distance and once something that looked like a deer. If we studied them and recorded any changes to their conditions, surely they might show us how humans would respond to the environment too?

There's very little in the library on this. There's very little on radiation poisoning in general – either in the library or in lessons. I asked Guardian Rich about it, but he paused to have a think and then just mumbled something about it being important that we had a broad education at this stage to stretch our minds and that the Mentors would teach us everything else we needed to know later. Anyway, in the end I kept looking and finally found a book in the library called *Chernobyl* and it talked all about this horrific nuclear accident in somewhere called the USSR and the impact of radiation poisoning on animals, including foxes, rats, rabbits and geese.

So this is what I talk about. I try to keep it short, logical and snappy; I don't want them to lose interest one minute in.

'In conclusion,' I say, 'scientists could set up designated animal feeding sites in the near Wilderness and trap and tag animals, thereby observing, over time, how their radiation sickness develops and whether there is any lessening of the symptoms. Thank you for listening.'

A massive toothy grin escapes.

Nailed it.

ARTHUR

I open two Cokes and pass one to Tommy. He raises an eyebrow.

'Nothing stronger?'

'It was your idea to help, remember?' I reply curtly. 'I can do this myself if you've changed your mind.' Tommy makes a suitably apologetic face and I press my index finger to the bottom right corner of the screen. System's on. I ignore the nine flashing messages – seven greens and two ambers – nothing that urgent. And now's not the time for distraction. I have to focus on this. I have to choose. I touch the Transition Centre icon, a face set within a capital C. It spins and I'm in.

The screen fills with the same backdrop as the opening to Father's speech – swirling neurons and morphing faces. The only significant difference is that this time there are no multiplying purple bacteria invading the screen. The consultant psychologists advised that consumers at the point of transition would not wish to be reminded of what was very probably the cause of their current body failure. Psychologists are among the very few people that Father respects and their hefty fees seem to only strengthen this regard. They spout the obvious and Father transfers the money, treating them all the while like modern-day seers.

I skip the introductory video in which a non-threateningly attractive brown-haired female scientist describes the process of selection. (She herself was carefully chosen. *People like to watch attractive people, but find extremely attractive people intimidating and less trustworthy; men are happier receiving information from women than other men; brunettes appear more intelligent than blondes – consultant bill £750,000, thank you very much for this razor-sharp input*).

I go straight to the 'set parameters' option and a drop-down menu appears. Up first is desired age. I select 17 to 20. Consumers are always advised to choose as close to the age of their Original as possible if they first 'die' young. A *stable* choice. Of course, if you're older there isn't the option. The maximum age is 30. There's too much cell deterioration after that. Plus, in Father's words, "The manufacturing costs are unsustainable." I think it's also that old people want to stay young. They have no desire to match their Original. The youthful exterior fits with 'how they feel inside'.

The '17' glows red and I scan my index finger once more to confirm I have clearance for an 'under 20' transition. The brain is only fully formed at 20, so there is a negligible risk of a minor data loss for an under 20 transition if the Original was older at the first time of passing. Under-sixteen isn't an option. The risks are too great. The likely outcome is that the Original's memories will be at least partially lost or corrupted and the new processor brain is scrambled and wasted. I remember a woman in an early AGM asking what she should do if her child got infected before the age of sixteen and Father replying with his typical tact: 'Don't let her die.'

I move onto the other parameters.

Gender: I click 'male' without hesitating and Tommy chuckles at my shoulder. I'd almost forgotten he was there.

Race: I click 'any'. 'Well, maybe you're not totally your father's son,' Tommy admits, still laughing. He's supposed to be helping, but I'm just finding his presence annoying.

IQ: I select 'over 130' and then scan my index finger again to gain access to the highest-level processors.

Hundreds of sub-options open up: eye colour, height, hair colour, hair texture, build. I let the cursor hover, but Tommy urges me to move on.

'Don't restrict yourself at this stage,' he advises. You'll just end up looking like your Original again. It seems to be hardwired into you as a default option and it's messing with your mind. Try something new. See what shows up.'

I follow his advice and leave all the selections blank. Next. Next. Next…

Three seconds later and the options begin to be displayed. Face after face stares out at me. Against all of

Tommy's advice I find myself instinctively clicking on a face that looks like my Original. Like the 'me' that I always expect to greet me in the mirror. Still.

4 – M3499. Caucasian. Same build. Similar height. Different eye colour. Blue to my green. Very respectable test scores. The summary reads 'a highly capable and visually pleasing processor with an aptitude for scientific data'. I tap on the most recent video clip. The Host is speaking about music; how regularly listening to classical music whilst revising can boost test scores. The voice is mellow. Nothing special, but it doesn't grate. Tommy mutes it after a few seconds, 'To make it easier to concentrate on the face. Make sure you're not going to be a squinter. Or a spitter. Jimmy's latest incarnation sprays a fine mist of spittle whenever he opens his mouth. Whilst this might be desirable if you're tending to an orchid, it's not so commendable when you're playing poker.' I don't laugh along. I block Tommy out and focus on the face. On my potential new face. No facial quirks. The face stays symmetrical whilst smiling and laughing. I move onto the next clip. Walking and running. The gait is even. The shoulders roll forwards as it picks up pace, but not in a way that stands out or would attract attention.

I turn to Tommy for his verdict.

'Fine,' he says neutrally. 'It's your life, so if that's what you want – fine.'

The obvious choice. An easy choice. All I need to do is click 'select' and book a date. But I don't do it. I run the video again. There's no spark. No light behind the eyes. I guess there won't be. They're not the same as us. Father always says it and his top scientists confirm it. We shouldn't project our emotions onto them.

I must have zoned out for a while as I suddenly seem to click back to reality and see Tommy's concerned face staring at me.

'What's going on in that tiny brain of yours?' he asks, his forehead creased with worry.

'Do you…' I begin and then stop. It's stupid.

'Do I what?' He won't let it go.

'Do you ever feel that we should … just die?' I ask, my voice little more than a whisper.

My mind goes to Mother on her deathbed. The smile on her gaunt face. Her voice calm as she explained why she wasn't going to transition.

'Immortality isn't a blessing,' she'd said. *'It's a curse. It is the fleeting nature of life that makes it special. It's like the seasons. If there were only summer it would lose its glow and you would pine for the cold.'*

Tommy listens. He doesn't shout at me like Father would. He doesn't tell me I'm feeble-minded. Instead he waits for me to finish and then stands in front of me, places his hands on my shoulders and forces me to look him in the eye.

74

'The Hosts are not like us. They don't suffer. Suffering requires pain and fear. Fear requires knowledge of one's fate and they are oblivious. So, no knowledge equals no suffering. Right up until the end. They have a comfortable life. They're fed, clothed, kept warm; they interact, they are educated. They even have a sense of purpose, of destiny, and absolute faith in a Creator. Every requirement of wellbeing is met. Moreover, they've never had parents. Will never have children. There's no one for them to fret over. No one to leave behind. Any DMW would take that life in a heartbeat.'

I nod but edge away, unconvinced.

I tell him that I have a headache coming on and that that's enough for this evening. That I'll keep looking tomorrow.

I decline his offer of another blue pill and show him out.

ALBA

The rain stings my eyes and scours my face, the wind driving it practically horizontal. I have the field to myself, everyone else choosing to stay indoors in the warmth. But I can't do that. There're no lessons today and days without lessons inch by without Curly. I tried moving from my room, to the library to the rec room but the tingling in my feet wouldn't stop. It built and built, an unscratchable itch. I needed to be out. To run.

As soon as I pick up pace, the anger starts to dissipate, the repeated impact of my feet against the tarmac track pounding the bad thoughts out of my brain. If Curly were still here she'd have made me kneel at the end of my bed and pray. That was her approach. Confess it all to the Creator and gain absolution and clarity. But she's not here, is she? I need to find my own coping mechanisms now.

I try to block all thoughts and just concentrate on the sound of my feet, the feeling of the rain. I look at the sky. It's monochrome, the rain not showing any sign of stopping soon. Approaching from the east is a flock of birds, a dark V against the grey. Poor things. They must have flown over swathes of Wilderness and will be suffering the final stages of radiation sickness. White patches from oxidative stress are the first stage. It was all in the *Chernobyl* book. White patches then cataracts, tumours, asymmetries and developmental abnormalities. They're flying closer and closer and I can feel my muscles stiffen and tighten. It's one thing reading about it in books when it's an interesting abstract concept. It's different in the flesh.

Please don't land. Please don't land.

Can you catch radiation sickness from birds? The Supervisor must think so as we're not allowed to leave food out that might tempt them. No picnics outside. Just in case. We hardly ever see any close up. And the dogs chase away any that approach.

Where are the dogs?

I'm in my head again and the bad thoughts crowd back in. I think of the fact that I've still had no word from Curly. Nothing. I think of the Morning Meeting and the latest selection. M2817. How could they have chosen M2817?!? OK, his face has perfect symmetry and his eyes are a rare amber colour. Guardians stare at him in the same way they used to look at Curly. Respect mixed with a kind of hunger. But the Mentors are supposed to be looking for people to help them cleanse the Wilderness for future humanity and his test scores are totally average. Not terrible. But average. Mine are far better. And all that

77

effort I put in for the last interview. Wasted. It makes no sense that a Mentor would choose him over anyone else. Over me. I sense my own ego and pick up pace. Outrunning the birds and the devil in my ear.

I repeat the Calming Mantra:

The Creator knows everything.

Everything happens for a reason.

But it doesn't help so I drive my legs faster and faster. I'm no longer a person. I'm moving pistons, a heartbeat, lungs. That's all. On my third lap of the track I have to stop. I'm gasping for breath and my side is killing. I double over, feeling the blood rush to my head. Above me, how high I can't tell, I start to feel the air vibrate and hum. My hair is whipped round my head and my ears pop. Disorientated, I rise in the midst of a mass of whirling wings and outstretched feet. The geese are landing. *Where the hell are the dogs?! The geese are landing!!!!*

My heart starts going crazy and I can't breathe. I literally can't breathe. They're poisoning me. I'm being poisoned. Close contact is all it takes. I'm breathing in radioactive air. Tiny particles will already be invading my bloodstream, attacking my cells. I try to scream but the scream stays lodged in my throat. A tumour. Decaying.

Now I'm on my knees, I don't know why – it's like the pressure, the knowledge that I'm dying is crushing me, forcing me to the floor – and I'm crawling away, the tarmac shredding my leggings. When I'm ten metres from the flock, I turn and force myself to look at them. My executioners. I'm ready for foaming mouths. For glazed-over eyes. For three legs and two beaks. But … there's nothing. I scan their feathers. They don't even have white spots. Instead, sleek black necks periscope in my direction. Black masks worn over white faces. Brown wings. Canada geese. I recognise them from the nature encyclopaedia.

They've flown over the Wilderness and they've survived. They're unharmed! It's a miracle!! A full-on bona-fide miracle. The sign we're all looking for. The cleansing is working! The Wilderness is ending!

A stupid smile threatens to pull my face apart and a bubble of laughter forms in my stomach and then explodes out of my mouth. I get to my feet, feeling like I might float away, and start heading to the side door, imagining all the Guardians' faces as I tell them.

'Don't go!' I shout at the geese. 'Don't go anywhere. You're my proof.'

'Ruhhh, ruh.'

The side door opens before I reach it and in a flash of white and brown, Dog 2 comes racing past me, gums pulled back in a snarl. The geese hiss their reply, snaking their necks from side to side, as they concede ground and retreat.

It's not enough to satisfy Dog 2.

'Ruhhhhhhhhhh.' His hind legs bend as he prepares to pounce.

'Come back, boy,' I call, trying to inject authority into my voice. 'Here. Heel. They're safe. They're fine.'

Dog 2 snarls again, baring sharp canines and the geese rise as a single unit.

I watch as they reform a V and disappear.

Dog 2 trots jauntily back inside, pride in his step, throwing a sideways glance at me as if to say, 'Job done.'

I don't need proof, I reassure myself.

I saw them.

I'm a witness. That's enough.

ARTHUR

The headache becomes real as I face the screen again.

I 'cancel' my 'current selection' and return to the original parameters. I feel like I'm slowly losing my mind. Tommy's right: if I'm going to keep my sanity, I need to make drastic changes.

Age: I leave as it is. 17 to 20.

Gender: I take a deep breath and click 'Female'.

The screen fills with faces, staring back out at me. Blonde, dark, redheads, brunettes. A paint palette of skin tones. How do they make me feel? Would I adjust better if I completely shunned my Original? If I wore one of these faces, would I finally find peace?

I click on a pale Redhead in the fifth row. Attractive, symmetrical face, widely spaced eyes and bow lips. Average IQ 131, averaged test score 88. There'd be no processing difficulties. I play the movement icon – fine. The breasts are large so move up and down in time with the legs. Presumably I'd get used to that. I press replay, searching myself for feelings of desire. That would overcomplicate things. None. But then again, desire isn't an emotion that troubles me much at the moment.

I click on the most recent interview – she's reciting a passage about the importance of friendship. The voice is warm, the cadence varied, but it doesn't move me. Following Tommy's example, I press the mute button. The mouth is symmetrical – no under or overbite. My eyes drift to hers. They're an unusual pale green and should have been striking, interesting, but somehow they aren't. They are just pale green. Washed out. Insipid.

I close the option and return to the main screen, scanning face after face. I open up four different options but quickly lose interest and close them again. I'm not sure what I'm looking for.

Until I find it. Row twelve, furthest to the right. 6 – F3527. Averaged test score 91. Attractive, but not remarkable. Wisps of hair escaping from a rather severe ponytail. A hint of tension in the face and shoulders raised a little too high and curved slightly in on themselves. All these details wash over me. I'm not looking at them. I'm looking at the eyes. They're an intense greeny-blue. But it's not even the colour that grabs me. Or the shape. Or the spacing. It's something harder to quantify but even harder to ignore.

These are eyes that see.

I'm aware of my pulse speeding up as I select the most recent interview clip. She's staring out the screen at me, almost daring me to look away, a smile dancing at the corner of her lips. I fast forward through the introductory questions and the maths until I reach the recital section. It's absurd, I'm know I'm projecting emotions onto her that she doesn't have, can't have, but I actually want to hear what she's chosen. When she names it – a poem – *The Brook* by Tennyson– my attention starts to falter. I'm expecting something pretty and trite. Beautiful sentiment but nothing more. But then she begins. Her delivery is straightforward. There's no great performance and she either doesn't pause for quite long enough at the end of the lines or she rushes it so the rhythm jars slightly, but there's an almost brutal innocence to it all. And the poem's words.

Men may come and men may go but I go on forever.

It's too much and I have to close the screen.

It's like she can see my soul. The nature of my existence.

That I don't come and go.

That I go on.

And on.

Forever.

ALBA

I stand outside the Guardians' rec room, shifting weight from one foot to the other, trying to pluck up the courage to knock at the door. Fragments of conversation and the occasional barrage of laughter escape through the crack between the door and the frame. What am I waiting for? I'm not in trouble for once. The reverse in fact. I have good news. Amazing news. So why won't the butterflies leave my stomach?

'Can I help you?' The icy voice of Guardian 12 steals up behind me. Damn. Not her. Why did it have to be her? She teaches us deportment. She's never liked me, always staring down her beak-like nose at me, brow furrowed in disappointment.

'Um. Yes, please can I speak to Guardian 9?'

'Any Guardian should be able to assist you. We are all equal before the Creator.'

'Guardian 9 asked me to come to see him.'

Guardian 12's eyes narrow slightly and the purple vein that snakes between her eyebrows expands and pulses.

'I see. Wait here.' She opens the door and then shuts it

quickly behind her, so all I get is a fleeting glimpse into a forbidden world.

It was a lie. Guardian 9 (call-me-Rich) hadn't asked to see me at all, and I didn't want to get him into trouble – I know that the other Guardians already think he is too friendly with us; smiles at us, talks in a normal voice rather than a bark. But I know I want it to be him I first tell about the geese. He listens at least, unlike the rest of them, and I want to be able to get out all the information without stumbling over my words or clamming up. Then we can take the news to the Supervisor together.

A few more minutes of staring at the wooden panelling and then Guardian Rich emerges, a couple of biscuit crumbs clinging to his beard as if he's saving them for later.

He's slightly on edge. He's pushing his round glasses further onto his nose even though they're not in any way falling off. He does this when he's nervous.

'Guardian R…' I burst out excitedly then realise that Guardian 12's still there – lurking just behind him, her face a picture of distrust. She knows something isn't right, she just isn't sure what.

'Guardian 9, I'm here as you requested,' I say, widening my eyes at the same time so that they're begging him to play along.

There's a pause. A fraction of a section pause and then call-me-Rich speaks.

'Ah, yes, thank you F3527. If you'll follow me…' His raised eyebrow is a question mark.

'Outside…' I add helpfully.

'Yes … outside, there's a job I'd like your assistance with.'

Guardian 12 frowns. She's still not satisfied but there's nothing she can do about it. I grin at Guardian Rich's broad back as I follow him all the way down the corridor and back out through the side door. It's good to know there are some people you can always count on. Who've got your best interests at heart and will never let you down.

Rich waits until we're both outside and the side door is firmly closed before speaking again.

'So, what's all this about?'

I can't help it, I'm basically hopping up and down with excitement, like I've been caught out, shoeless, on hot tarmac at midday.

'Geese. It's about geese. Geese that I saw here. This morning. And we're going to be OK. It's all OK.'

I take in Rich's confused face and I realise I'm rambling, spewing forth information and making no sense and I think that maybe I need some visual aids.

'Here,' I burble, gesturing to the point on the track where the geese had landed, a single white and brown feather left on the ground like a place marker. 'Or maybe fractionally to the right, but close enough. A whole flock of them. And they were perfectly healthy. Their eyes were clear, their feathers weren't discoloured at all, no mottling, no patches, no feather loss, nothing.' I pick up the feather and roll the stem between my right thumb and index finger.

'Look, it's fine. I can touch it and I'm fine.' My feet are dancing again.

Call-me-Rich doesn't speak immediately. He's staring at the ground, as if he can derive clues from the tarmac. When he finally looks up his voice is quiet and hesitant.

'…Maybe you couldn't see clearly enough from where you were standing.'

'No,' I say impatiently. 'I was right next to them. I could see everything.'

This wasn't going how I'd imagined. Not at all. He was supposed to be excited. Why wasn't he excited? I know my discovery's enormous/serious/massive – pick an adjective – with implications beyond anything I've studied. And that it might take a while to process, and we wouldn't be dancing and whooping the first minute. But he wasn't even tapping his toe. He wasn't even smiling.

'Different species exhibit different symptoms of radiation poisoning,' he offered.

'But these were Canada geese. I've read about them in the library. I know the symptoms and they didn't have any.'

'Maybe they'd only just been infected so the symptoms weren't showing yet?'

'No, no,' I say, my voice rising, tainted with anger. Why was he deliberately not believing me? 'I said the geese came from the east, remember? That's the Wilderness. All the way to the coast. We did it in Geography. They'd have flown over hundreds of miles of it. If it's as bad out there as everyone says it is, the geese would be sick, wouldn't they? They'd have to be? So – don't you see?! The radiation must have lifted! And if geese are OK, humans might be too! We might not need to be here any more! We can leave. We can all leave!'

Rich's demeanour suddenly changes gear and it's like he's been possessed.

'Stop it. Stop talking,' he hisses. *'Now.'* He's no longer looking at me. His eyes are scanning the yard, wildly, as if searching out potential eavesdroppers. No one's there. Attention back on me, he grabs my shoulders, pulling me close and bending his knees so that his eyes are directly level with mine. His are grey and I think of thunderstorms.

'Don't tell anyone else about this, Alba.' His voice is low and rough and harsher than I've ever heard it. 'Don't tell the Supervisor or the other Guardians or the students or anyone. Do you understand?'

I can smell his breath – stale with notes of coffee and

lemon shortbread – and I try to pull away, but his hands only grip more tightly.

'What's going on?' I ask. I can feel the downy hairs on the back of my neck start to stand up and my throat constrict. 'What aren't you telling me?'

'Promise me!'

His fingers are digging deeper into my muscle and I'm backing away, head down. I don't want to be here any more. Everything in my body is saying run. I don't want to be here with this man saying these things and not smiling about the geese.

He releases one hand from my shoulder and I think here's my chance, but then he wraps it round my chin, pulling my jaw up, forcing my eyes to meet his again.

I stare at him defiantly, expecting to see anger, but finding only fear. And concern.

For me.

'Alba…' It's like the word is torn out of him. *'Promise me.'*

'OK,' I murmur and he lets go of me and just stands there. Shoulders and knees turned in. Back hunched. A desiccated version of his former self. I drop the feather and watch it spiral away on the breeze.

ARTHUR

It's 2am and Tommy's messaging me. He wants to plan my New Body Party and needs to know how I feel about a Hawaiian theme.

I don't answer. His question annoys me. New Body Parties are certainly practical – you need to show your new incarnation to your friends so they can continue to recognise you, but I've always found the 'party' element somehow distasteful. And Tommy's the only real friend I have. To pass unrecognised amongst the rest would be a godsend.

Tommy won't be offended by my lack of response – he'll think I'm asleep – he knows I'm no night owl like he is. And I'm not in the mood to talk to him. I can never keep anything from Tommy – I try, but he sees straight through me. He's always been the more rational one, the more detached. He can observe the world as if through a lens and smile his lopsided grin that the girls, and boys, somehow find so irresistible. But the world isn't governed by logic and reason alone. If it were, there'd be no need for poetry, for novels, for songs.

I'm at my computer again. Looking at her again. I

couldn't sleep so I gave up trying and decided to watch the rest of the interview instead.

I try to justify it to myself on the basis that transitioning is an important decision. It's only natural that it should prey on my mind and eat away at my thoughts. But deep down I know it's more than that.

I can't endure the poem again and the gulf of emotions it prompted so I fast-forward through it to reach the Personal Statement. I have to know what she's chosen to talk about. It is more than curiosity. It is a thirst that must be slaked. The time stamp on the video reads 5:03 and I press play.

My muscles stiffen as I catch the last half line of the poem: *I go on forever*, but then relax as she finishes and pauses, inhaling deeply as if readying herself for a daunting task. Her whole face changes. The expression intensifies and her eyebrows knit together as if to underline the importance of what she is going to say next.

'For my Personal Statement I would now like to talk about a possible alternative approach to monitoring radiation levels...'

Her voice is serious and controlled, but her eyes sparkle with energy and determination and her hands won't keep still. One rarely sees a host's hands during a seated interview. They are normally placed in the lap, docile, resting. But her hands keep popping into frame, emphasising points, fingers almost bursting free of palms as she talks about trapping, tagging and monitoring animals in the near Wilderness.

My finger shakes as I press pause. For a second time her interview has left me feeling winded. A blow to the solar plexus. Obviously, I knew a world had been built around them. A world with its own set of rules and mythology. Its own explanations for their confinement, for their solitude. 'An enabling world' was the title of the psychologists' report. I remember it sitting on Father's desk. I never read it. I told myself that it wasn't my area. My focus has always been looking for new antibiotics and then when that went nowhere, on research into vaccines. Cures or protection that could be available to all. Work that meant my internal monologue could label me a 'good person … nothing like his father'. I've heard the report summarised at Board Meetings and AGMs and thought that was enough. *A world system that has inbuilt mythical structures to enable the Hosts to live fulfilling existences with a sense of purpose. To prevent them from questioning their confinement and experiencing the debilitating effects of doubt and worry.*

But seeing the lie presented here, in this way. The Wilderness. Mentors. Radiation. To see her grappling her way through it, spurred on by hope, throws everything into doubt. They're not meant to question. They're not meant to suffer.

They're not meant to be like us.

And the worst thing about it, the very worst, is that a little part of me must have known what was going on. I've always thirsted for knowledge so why was I content with the scraps of a summary? Why hadn't I queried what these 'inbuilt mythical structures' were? I had been wilfully blind. A child who turns its head so they do not have to face an unpleasant truth. Eats meat but would never butcher an animal.

I start to feel dizzy and feverish so I head to the bathroom to splash some water on my face. The sickness recedes but then I remember the hatred in the eyes of the man in the mask as he hurled an egg at me. I raise my face to the basin mirror and his eyes become my own.

Murderer.

Dabbing my face dry with a towel, I steel myself. I can't look away any more. I return to my computer and press play.

Just over eight minutes into the interview, the feed starts to pixelate and then cuts out, the screen turning black. I refresh and fast-forward from the beginning. The same thing happens – at 8:12 the screen pixelates and then it goes dark. I restart the computer, restart the router. The same thing happens. A wave of irritation builds and crashes over me, causing me to slam my hand against the desk. I want to hear the rest of what she has to say.

I return to the menu and click on the 'report a fault'

button. A comment box materialises and I type in 'request reinterview of 6 – F3527 due to technical issues with the recording' and enter my status code. I won't be refused. The one good thing about being the heir to the M.A.D.E. corporation – I never am.

ALBA

I wake feeling groggier than normal. We had to sleep with the windows closed again because the wind had changed direction and was now blowing from the Wilderness. The lack of fresh air always clouds my head.

I sit by myself at breakfast. The table in the corner with the uneven legs that everyone always avoids. Same as at dinner last night. I'm on edge and I don't trust anyone. I see and feel eyes where there aren't any, staring at me, waiting for me to trip up.

Don't tell anyone else about this, Alba.

Promise me.

Guardian Rich's words echo on repeat in my head and my brain whirrs round and round trying to work out what I've done wrong and why they don't want me to know that the radiation is clearing. Why they don't want anyone to know. I must be right, after all. I held the feather. I held the feather with my bare skin and I'm fine. No blistering. No sickness. Nothing.

I'm staring at my porridge, pushing around the raisins on top, trying to dull my thoughts. To focus instead on its texture, the undulations, the beige blandness of it all.

Suddenly there's a sharp tap on my shoulder. I swivel round to meet the upright frame, beak nose and cold eyes of Guardian 12.

My windpipe narrows. What does she want from me? Does she know I know?

'You're needed in Interview Room 1.' Her voice is reassuringly disinterested, but I still sense a trap.

'But… I recorded on Tuesday?'

'There was a technical error halfway through,' she replies. 'Someone reported a fault.'

I follow her down the corridor, not bothering to try and keep pace. Her feet tap, tap, tap against the polished floorboards. A jaunty rhythm. As if nothing's wrong. As if this place isn't full of liars and frauds and friends who leave and forget you.

She unlocks the door of Interview Room 1, points at the chair in the centre by way of instruction and then seems to take in my appearance for the first time.

'Goodness, F3527. You cannot record looking like this.'

I instinctively raise my hand to my head, and my fingers meet tangles. I didn't brush my hair this morning. Or my teeth, for that matter. It didn't seem important. Nothing does. Guardian 12 opens the bottom draw of the technician's desk and produces a comb and hair band with a flourish.

'For emergencies such as these,' she declares, grabbing

a handful of hair with one wiry hand and proceeding to brush, or rather pull, it out by its roots with the other.

I squeal and squirm but she ignores me, finally tying my hair up in a ponytail so severe that it raises my eyebrows about a centimetre up my forehead.

'Wait here while I fetch a technician.'

I sit in the chair, kicking the central metal pole with the soles of my shoes, enjoying the discordant 'gong' sound it makes. What's the point? Record for what? For Mentors who don't care? Because Guardians who pretend to be our friend but are actually all complicit in some big weird conspiracy tell us to?

Maybe I won't speak. Won't say anything at all. It wouldn't matter. They'd choose someone else anyway. Like last time. Someone *prettier*. I start to spin the chair. Round and round so the colours swirl and blend. But then, mid-spin, it strikes me. Someone reported an error. And requested a rerecord. Which means that someone was watching. Me. My interview. And wanted to hear the rest of what I had to say. So maybe Guardian Rich was wrong... Maybe he's just old and scared of new ideas, which is why he's here and not in the Research City. Maybe the Scientists there are much more open-minded. Maybe they'd want to know if the Wilderness is changing. If they wanted to hear the rest of my animal theory then surely they'd want to know about the geese? They'd know what to do. What it all meant. I feel my heart rate accelerating and energy leaving my core and starting to fill my limbs again. My brain is buzzing, drugged by this new sense of purpose.

Bang.

The door is flung open and my thoughts are interrupted by the reappearance of Guardian 12, propelling a young technician into the room in front of her. He has thin, lank hair and glasses that are so strong they completely distort his face. I haven't met him before. Maybe he's transferred in from another Home. I know this isn't the only one.

'No need for the poem or any preliminaries this time,' Guardian 12 barks at the technician, ignoring me. 'Just straight to the Personal Statement. Watch the sound levels for clarity.' She shakes her head and lets out a dry little laugh as if this is the most ridiculous thing ever. 'And for goodness' sake don't mess this one up.'

The technician nods his acknowledgment and then swallows, sending his Adam's apple rippling forwards and backwards in his overly long neck.

Guardian 12 leaves and the red light on the camera starts to flash on and off. I can feel my adrenaline levels spiking.

'Ready?' the technician asks.

'Yes,' I reply firmly and the light stops flashing and stays a steady red.

I'm ready.

I talk for seven minutes and thirty-three seconds about the geese. About their landing, their general health, my touching a feather without suffering any noticeable side effects and the enormous implications of it all.

'Thanks for listening,' I conclude before sitting back in the chair, shoulders meeting upholstery. I hadn't realised I'd been leaning forwards the whole time.

I don't smile as I wait for the red light to go out. The confidence and elation I was feeling moments earlier is receding. Flowing into the floor, earthed like static electricity through a conducting strip.

I remember the fear on Guardian Rich's face, and shiver.

Don't tell anyone.

Promise me.

Have I done the right thing?

Or have I just made a huge mistake?

ARTHUR

'So, a girl this time? Right. Didn't think you had it in you.'
Tommy lets out a throaty chuckle of amusement.

'She's different,' I bite back.

'Of course.' Tommy's still smiling, laughter glinting at
the edges of his eyes.

'Mind if I?' He nods towards the coffee machine sitting
on the kitchen island. 'You've woken me hellishly early so
the least you can do is caffeinate me properly. You?'

I decline his offer and watch as the machine purrs black
espresso into a cup. He takes a sip, gives himself an
exaggerated shake awake and then follows me into the
living room.

He sits back in the sofa. I remain standing.

'So, aren't you going to show me?'

I start to move towards the computer on the desk in the
corner and then stop myself. He doesn't need to see to
understand. I can tell him. About the poem. About the
geese. How she's figuring it all out. That will be enough.
I don't want to *show* her to him. Have him judge her. Mute
her voice and then comment on the symmetry of her
mouth movements. Click back on a different video and

watch her breasts rise and fall as she walks. It seems … degrading. But it's not just about protecting her. At the back of my mind I'm aware of a little voice saying, *I don't want to share her.*

As I talk, I find myself starting to pace. To the window and back. Up and down, up and down, and with every repetition, my living room, large by any conventional standards, seems to shrink and become increasingly claustrophobic. I need Tommy's support on this. I need him to understand. My breathing becomes shallower and shallower, as if my lungs are also aware of a rapidly dwindling volume of air.

'It's like she's the only one awake,' I conclude. 'You were wrong. We were all wrong. They're not different to us. They have the same emotional depth. The same capacity for suffering. Just because they have numbers rather than names. Just because they were grown in a lab. It doesn't mean they aren't human.'

I stare at Tommy, waiting for a eureka moment that never comes.

'Arthur, old chap,' Tommy's voice is overly reasonable and it grates. He continues, unaware, 'It's completely normal to project emotions like this. People do it all the time. We view every creature in our own image and imbue it with our own characteristics. *My dog's head is open in the approximation of a smile, its tongue lolling out – it must be laughing.* No, it's panting to reduce body heat. *The monkey is scratching its head – it must be pondering a difficult question.* No, most likely it has fleas.'

'Tommy … she's a girl. She's not a dog or a monkey. She's a girl.' My voice is a warning growl. 'Haven't you listened to anything I've said?'

'But this *girl*,' Tommy draws out the word playfully, as if stretching it between his teeth, 'she hasn't worked out any fundamental truths about us – she's found a poem about a brook in a book and recited it.'

'What about the geese?'

'From your description it again doesn't seem particularly remarkable. She's performed some basic logical deductions. Any computer could do the same. The hosts are screened for this. If they can't process, they're no use, are they?'

I stay at the other end of the room. I want to distance myself from Tommy as much as I can. He suddenly seems toxic.

'How can you … just say…' Anger attacks my sentences, fragmenting them, turning them into shards that lodge in my throat.

'Look, Arthur,' Tommy's tone has shifted. It's gentle now, sincere. 'I get that she's had an impact on you. That something about her reminds you of your mother and that's clouding your judgement. The tumour…'

'This is not about the tumour…'

'Are you sure? Days are passing. Paranoia, problems with reasoning. These are all symptoms. Dr Peters said so, I remember you telling me. When we're out you're always looking over your shoulder as if someone's following you.'

'They are!' I exclaim and then bite my tongue. I'm not helping myself. 'This is not about the tumour,' I repeat through gritted teeth. 'Just watch the interview, OK? Then you'll see.'

'That's what I originally suggested,' he counters.

I turn on my computer. I have no choice.

I open the screen, log in and pull up my recent views. There's the male who looks too similar to my Original. The redhead female with the washed-out green eyes. The brunette. But no 6 – F3527.

It must be another technical malfunction.

I open the search engine and begin to type.

6 – F3527.

No results.

My left eyeball starts to shake.

'Try searching by Centre number,' Tommy suggests.

It takes me a second to remember that the number before the F or M refers to the Centre that the host is located in. I type Centre 6 into the box.

The screen fills with faces and I scroll down. And down again. And again. Until I reach the end of the last page.

'She's gone,' I say slowly.

'Maybe someone else has selected her?' Tommy ventures.

But no, that couldn't be it, could it? I last watched the video less than eight hours ago. Hosts aren't usually taken off the system until at least twelve hours after selection in case there is a change of mind.

I stagger away from my desk. There's a lightness in my head and I lean for support on the top of the nearest armchair. It's velvet and all I can think is that it's the softest thing I've ever touched and as long as I just think about that, the softness, and nothing else, I might stay standing.

'Arthur,' Tommy asks quietly, concern filling his eyes. 'Are you sure she was ever actually there?'

'Of course she was,' I reply.

She must have been.

I couldn't have imagined her, could I?

And then I stop thinking about the softness of the velvet and I hit the floor.

ALBA

'F3527!'

Guardian 8's voice booms out across the vegetable patches and I look up from my task thinning the cabbage seedlings to see him striding in my direction, blonde fringe swept back by the wind.

Anger is radiating off him, from his overly wide eyes to the way he is squaring his shoulders to his rolling gait, and I thank the Creator that he's not carrying his gun. My stomach contracts. It might not be the video, I tell myself. It might be anything. A reported failure to wash my hands properly, sustained contact with a male student. I did talk to M2993 in the library for ten minutes. It was about a book, but someone might have seen and said something. Just look at the floor, I coach myself silently. When a Guardian gets like this, riled up, it's best to be submissive. To look at the floor and avoid eye contact. Just do what they say and stay quiet.

I stand up and shuffle towards him, head bowed. Butterflies are dancing in my stomach. No, it doesn't feel like butterflies. The movements are harsher. It's more like locusts. Swarming.

They normally just tell you to walk behind them, but this time he grabs my elbow, twisting it. I bite back a scream.

'What have you done? What the hell have you done??'

Everyone has stopped work now and is just staring at us, trowels raised, weeds held mid-air. Eyes boring, tunnelling, trying to dig for secrets.

Guardian 8 swivels back towards the main building, pulling me alongside him. His legs are one and a half times as long as mine and I have to jog to keep pace.

Back inside, he drags me down the main corridor and then right, up a side staircase that's normally out of bounds to us. He's not saying anything and I'm too scared to ask.

I know it's not about hand washing.

I know it's not about a boy.

We pass Guardian Rich coming down in the other direction and his face says it all.

What have you done? What have you done?

At the top of the stairs, Guardian 8 propels me down side corridor after side corridor – twisting and turning, taking us deeper into the labyrinth. Finally, he stops outside a solid-looking dark grey door.

'Your new home,' he says, mouth twisting to one side. 'While the Supervisor works out what's to be done with you.'

Guardian 8 unhooks a bunch of keys from his belt, rifles

through them and produces a large one with a triangular head. He inserts it into the lock. The door opens to reveal a cramped, cell-like room. There is a tiny window at the top of the far wall, letting in a slither of sky, a single wire-framed bed and a basin and metal toilet in the corner.

My skin feels like it's wrapped in spiders' webs.

'You're to stay here until the Supervisor's ready for you.'

He turns. His jacket strains at the back, the slit revealing a triangle of striped shirt.

'What have I done?' I ask in a shaking voice.

Guardian 8 ignores me. The door slams and he's gone.

The room is dark. I sit on the bed, wrap my arms round my knees and stare at the door.

All the doors in the classrooms have glass panels. The dorms too. *The Creator sees everything.* Curly and I used to joke that the Guardians liked to watch us sleep. It's annoying in the summer as the light can stream in that way, bypassing the blackout blinds. But on the whole I like it. It means you never feel completely isolated. Like this.

'What have I done?' I repeat quietly to myself. But this time it's not a question. I know what I've done. I ignored Guardian Rich and talked about the geese.

And now I'm here. Alone.

Totally and utterly alone.

And further away from the Research City and Curly than I've ever been.

ARTHUR

The first time I approach M.A.D.E. Head Office's revolving doors I lose my nerve halfway through and do a 360 rotation, exiting the way I came.

I berate myself for my cowardice. She exists. I'm certain of it. She exists and for some reason they're hiding her away. Keeping her from me. Or, Tommy's right and I'm losing my mind. This is the only way to find out for sure which it is.

Steeling myself, I make it through the doors on the second attempt and approach the reception desk.

'Good morning, Mr Easton,' Ellie, the receptionist, smiles, focusing her 100-watt smile on me. 'How may I assist you today?'

'I'm here to see Father,' I reply.

'Very good, I'll let Linda know you're here.'

There's a pause as she puts in a call to the eighth floor.

'Oh, Mr Easton, there seems to be some confusion. They weren't expecting you today.'

'This wasn't scheduled. It's important though.'

'Of course.'

'I'll just head up.'

I start to head across the lobby.

'Mr Easton, er ... Mr Easton...'

The smile dims and then flickers off. Ellie, along with every other M.A.D.E. employee knows how much Father hates to be disturbed, but I'm at the lifts before anyone can stop me. Ted, the security guard is looking over, sensing that something isn't quite right, but he's not going to risk manhandling the heir to the most powerful man in the country. I step inside, press level 8 and press my finger against the security panel. Only directors are allowed up to level 8.

The lift pings its arrival and the doors open to reveal Linda, Father's secretary, ready to intercept me.

'Arthur, lovely to see you. How are you? Perhaps we could schedule an appointment for later in the week?'

'This can't wait, I'm afraid.'

I dodge round her, and approach Father's door. There's no sound coming through it. Looks like he's not in with anyone.

Heart thumping in my chest, I knock on the door and then enter before he has a chance to respond.

The obligatory count of three before he deigns to look up.

'Arthur.'

A treatise of condemnation is condensed into a single word.

'Father...' My left eyeball is threatening to wobble. I will it to stay still, focusing on my prepared speech.

'I wish to visit Centre 6.'

Father shuffles papers, disinterested.

'I'm pleased you've finally picked a host, Arthur, but you don't need my permission to transition. Just make the appointment.'

'No, that's not it,' I reply. 'I wish to visit a host in Centre 6.'

Father sits back in his armchair. This is the first time in my life that I have seen him look surprised. It's not an emotion he wears well.

'And,' he says, trying to regain his usual composure, 'why, might I ask, is this?'

I launch the first strand of my attack.

'I cannot decide which of two hosts to choose between. They are both located in Centre 6. I thought it might facilitate my choice.'

'I see.' He is softening, his eyebrows descending. My apparent willingness to arrange transition placating his ire. '…It is unusual though.'

Time for the second strand.

'And, I've been thinking about what you said…' I hesitate – Father will expect some hesitation. 'I want to become more involved in the family business. As you said, research into new vaccines is yielding little in the way of results. I thought I might be of greater help if I got to understand every element of the process. And touring the inside of a Centre seems a logical step. You see very little from the basement alone.'

Father smiles and the tension leaves his face. It's amazing how flattery can dull the brain of even the cleverest man.

'Right. Very good.' He is moments away from rubbing his hands with glee. 'I'll update your clearance levels. Centre 6, you say?' He thinks for a moment. 'That's only an hour and a half away. You can be there and back in a day.'

I turn to leave.

'Oh and Arthur.'

'Yes.'

'I'm so pleased you've seen sense over this. Maybe you're a chip off the old block after all.'

ALBA

Guardian 11 brings in breakfast at seven. A bowl of already-cold porridge on a tray. He didn't wake me. I wasn't asleep. Didn't sleep all night. Well, that's not entirely true. I must have slept for a while as I remember jerking awake from a nightmare. There was a screen. I was watching myself on a screen. I was tiny – little more than a speck in the middle. I was trying to talk about the geese but I was too small and the volume was too low so no one could hear. And then it wasn't me watching, it was Curly. Curly watching and reaching into the screen and crushing me between her forefinger and thumb. The rest of the night I stared at the wall and tried to think of nothing.

Guardian 11 doesn't stay. He just puts the tray down in the corner of the room, together with a fresh dress, hairbrush, a pocket mirror and toothbrush and tells me, in his deep, gravelly voice, to be ready in an hour.

'Ready for what?' I ask.

He doesn't answer and I hear the lock click shut again on the outside as he leaves.

I go to the tray and pick up the bowl and try to force myself to eat. To focus on daily chores, one at a time.

Using rituals to overcome the waves of fear that are threatening to capsize me. The porridge tastes even worse without the distraction of conversation.

Then I dress. The clothes feel starched and sit off my skin, as if they're trying to avoid contact. I flip open the pocket mirror and flinch. My face looks even paler than normal and the eyes sit hollow and haunted. My hair's a wild mess but I don't care. I tie it up into a ponytail and then sit at the end of the bed and wait. Seconds elongate and time seems to stretch. Elastic.

Eventually there's the sound of the key in the lock again and Guardian 11's back.

'She's ready to see you now.'

I don't bother to ask who 'she' is. His tone says it all.

The Supervisor.

I've brushed my teeth but it doesn't cut through the bile rising up my throat and my mouth tastes more metallic than minty as I follow Guardian 11 back through the maze of passageways. My eyes squint as we reach the main downstairs corridor, readjusting to the bright strip lighting. Students we pass avert their eyes as if they can sense I'm somehow contaminated. Toxic.

The door to the Supervisor's private office is bright yellow. A happy colour, supposedly. I don't know anyone who's been happy to be sent here. This morning the colour seems to mock me. Guardian 11 pushes the door and we're through to the section where the Supervisor's Assistant sits. There's a small desk which she perches behind, birdlike, but no other chairs. Just a carpeted space before another door, grey this time, all pretence at happiness now dropped. We stand and my legs start to shake.

The intercom on the assistant's desk buzzes.

'You can go in now, she's expecting you,' the assistant chirps. She looks at Guardian 11 and then her eyes dart towards mine, unable to disguise their curiosity, then flit away again.

Guardian 11 raps sharply at the door before twisting the handle and bundling me inside.

A chair is set out in the centre of the room, ready. It's grey plastic, low without arms, a deliberate contrast to the padded burgundy leather armchair the Supervisor is ensconced in behind her heavy desk. The Supervisor's eyes flick over at me and then at the chair. I sit. Guardian 11 stays behind me, by the door. I'm on alert. A cornered animal. All exits blocked.

The Supervisor still hasn't spoken. Instead her fingers are drumming a rhythm on the desk's polished surface. *Brrrruuummm. Brrrruummmm.* It goes straight through me, making my cells vibrate. *Brrruummmmmm. Brrruummmm.* I hadn't noticed her fingers before. They're large. Too large for her hands. Thick like cabbage stalks. *Brrruummmmmm. Brruummmmm.*

Abruptly the drumming stops and she leans forward, torso almost crawling across the desk towards me.

'Who have you told?' The red lipstick is designed to make her lips look bigger but it doesn't work. It only thins them further. To a tiny red circle. A gun's muzzle. The words are bullets, fired towards me.

'I ... um ... I don't understand,' I stammer back.

'About the geese. Who have you told?'

'No one,' I reply, quickly. It's the truth. 'No one at all.'

'No one at all...' she mimics, throwing the words back in my face. She bark laughs as her eyes flash. 'No one at all... Guardian 11...' Guardian 11 makes a hesitant noise of acknowledgement, a sort of deep cough laugh, wary of involvement. 'Would you call a video, broadcast to the entire...' she pauses for a moment, 'Research City, no one at all?'

'Certainly not.' Guardian 11 shakes his head vigorously, seemingly relieved at the ease of the question.

I could hear Curly in my head coaching me to be quiet and subservient. To sit up straight, say the bare minimum. I ignored her.

'I thought they'd be interested,' I say, my voice wavering but managing to meet the Supervisor's eye for the first time. 'Interested that the radiation is lifting. That the Wilderness is becoming safe again.'

'Stop it,' she hisses. 'Stop it. You don't know what you're

115

saying. You're an ignorant little girl who knows nothing and has come up with some ridiculous theory.'

It's not a ridiculous theory, I want to shout. What other interpretation is there? But there's something about the way she's looking at me, like I am a bug she's deciding whether or not to crush that makes me swallow the words.

The phone on her desk rings once but she silences it.

'Have you told F3106? F3114?'

I shake my head. And look at the floor. Force my face and body language to be as neutral as possible. Only the Creator knows what's going to happen to me. I try to forget that I can no longer feel my hands and instead work on not taking anyone down with me.

'F2991?'

Name after name. She fires them at me, observing me for any trace of guilt, any involuntary flinch, looking for further victims, for co-conspirators.

'M2993?'

The phone on her desk rings again, but she continues to ignore it.

Finally, the names stop. A glimmer of relief gives way to further panic. What now? What are they going to do with me now?

'Guardian 11, please contact M.A.D.E. Head Office requesting emergency transition.'

'Of course,' Guardian's 11's face is sombre.

'And we might need another Guardian in here.

Emergency transition? Another Guardian? They're talking about me and I know it's really bad. It's really, really bad. But I've got no idea what they're talking about. My throat's constricting and I'm struggling to breathe. I need to get out of here.

'What's going on?' I ask, quietly.

The Supervisor ignores me.

My nerves are firing and muscles tensing as I rise to standing. It's now or never. With a bound, I lunge for the door, but before I reach it, Guardian 11's there and he's got my arms and is twisting them behind my back and I'm screaming.

The phone rings again and her assistant's face is at the now open door frame, creased in urgency.

'I'm sorry, Supervisor, but you really need to take this call…'

With a low growl, the Supervisor picks the receiver up in a white-knuckled grasp.

'Yes?'

Tiny bits of spittle hit the receiver and pool.

Then something the person on the other end says punctures her anger and replaces it with something I've never seen there before.

Fear.

She inhales deeply as if to reinflate.

'Mr Easton, this is an honour. And what can we do for you?

ARTHUR

I'm angry now. Seething. I feel the heat of it radiating from my pores. The only way I'm going to determine whether F3527 actually exists or is a tumour-induced hallucination is to speak to Centre 6's Supervisor, but she's rejecting my calls. Her ineffectual assistant with the wheedling voice keeps saying she's putting me through but then the line goes dead again.

'I'm terribly sorry, Mr Easton, but she's in a meeting,' she grovels for the second time.

'Then get her out of the meeting,' I reply. My voice is calm but with steel edges. I've learnt from Father how best to harness anger. How to make it slice and cut.

'I'm trying again, sir…'

There's a longer pause, a crackle, the indistinct murmur of a distant conversation and then a different voice on the line. Harsher, more authoritative.

'Yes?'

It's the Supervisor.

I reconnect with my anger and sharpen the blade.

'My name is Arthur Easton. Director of M.A.D.E. and son of Michael Easton.

The silence on the other end of the line tells me that my importance has been registered.

'Mr Easton, this is an honour. And what can we do for you?' she wheezes.

'I wish to visit Centre 6.'

'...It is best to arrange a transition through the normal channels, sir,' comes the reply.

'No.' I let my impatience show. 'I do not want to arrange a transition, I wish to *visit* the Centre.'

'Visit?' echoes the voice, thrown. 'That is ... somewhat unorthodox ... but can, of course, be arranged. Is there ... any reason for your interest?'

I inhale sharply. I cannot let my voice waver. I cannot show any sign of doubt or weakness. 'I wish to enquire about a certain Host, F3527.'

There's a pause. A long pause this time. I can tell her words are being chosen and weighed before being enunciated.

'I wish to reassure you, Mr Easton, that the matter is in hand. The Host has had no contact with the other Hosts and every trace of her has been removed from the servers. We are in the process of arranging an emergency transition. It is an extremely regrettable but contained incident for which I can only profusely apologise.'

I don't concentrate on her words. Just the substance. And suddenly I'm floating. I'm not crazy. She exists. The girl who can see *exists*. A smile dances on my face and I fight it out of my voice.

'Do not arrange for transition.'

'I'm sorry?'

'I said do not arrange for transition.'

'… as you wish.'

'It is not a wish. It is an order.' I want there to be no doubts, no room for error. 'I…' my voice threatens to crack. 'I want to meet her.'

The line crackles and I hear a sharp intake of breath.

'… apologies but the line is quite bad this end. Please could you repeat yourself?'

'I am coming to meet her. Later today. Twelve-ish.' The last words tumble out of my mouth, chasing each other, as if aware I might be tempted to bite them back in.

There's a long pause followed by a clipped, 'Right.' There's a coldness to the voice and suddenly I'm fearful for F3527. For her safety. Suppose the Supervisor decides to dispose of her anyway? Punishes her for my phone call. My intrusion into her kingdom. I cannot let that happen.

'The standard of care afforded to Hosts is of utmost importance to M.A.D.E. executives,' I say, every word enunciated staccato. 'I trust I will not be disappointed by what I see at Centre 6.'

'No, sir. Certainly not.' The deference is back. The fear resurfacing.

'Till twelve then.'

'Twelve.'

ALBA

The Supervisor replaces the receiver and then looks at me. Her whole manner's different. She's on edge. Wary. Of me. There is no mention of my attempted escape. No more talk of 'emergency transition', whatever that might be. When Guardian 11 lets go of my arms and pushes me back onto the chair, she admonishes him with a barked, 'Gentle!'

Stalking round to the front of her desk she rests her thighs against it and then leans forwards until her eyes are level with mine.

'In two hours a very important man is coming to see you,' she says seriously. 'It is imperative that you respond to his questions with respect. That you show suitable deference. And that you display gratitude for all the comforts and care you have enjoyed here.'

I stay silent.

Her eyes rake me up and down and her mouth puckers as if she's tasted something sour.

'He will also expect you to look…' she waves her hand in the air as if to supply the missing words. *Not. Like. That.*

'Repeat to me the Creator's Fourth Commandment.'

I say nothing, but continue to stare at her. The power balance has shifted. I can feel it. The air seems to shudder with static electricity and I barely suppress a smirk. Her hand twitches, itching to strike me. Instead she supplies the answer to her own question.

'*A smart appearance reflects a smart mind.* Take this time to prepare yourself, physically and mentally. You're dismissed. But make no mistake,' her customary sneer returns, 'we will be watching you at all times.'

'Shall I return her to Block 4?' Guardian 11 asks from behind my shoulder.

'No.' The Supervisor pauses as she thinks. 'Take her to G3. And send someone to help her get ready.'

* * *

I'm back in a room alone again, but it couldn't be more different from the last one. It's on the other side of the building, next to the Guardians' sleeping quarters. The mattress is soft. Not collapsing-broken-spring-soft like some of the dorm beds are, rather it moulds to your body when you lie down, cocooning you. I don't trust it.

The room has its own private shower off it and I stand under the hot jet, chin raised, eyes closed, letting the water pummel my face. On a little shelf inside the shower sit vials of shower gel, shampoo and conditioner. They smell of mint and rosemary and the fragrance binds with the steam and rises.

I'm about to meet a Mentor. I must be, there's no other explanation. And a senior one at that, or the Supervisor wouldn't be acting so weird. Someone who's been across the Wilderness. Who lives in the Research City. Someone who might even have met Curly. So why do the flutters in my stomach not feel like excitement?

And why was he coming? Mentors never normally meet potential Apprentices. They watch our videos and scrutinise our exam results and then choose from afar. Was he coming because I'd impressed him? Or was he coming because I was somehow dangerous? To destroy me? And would he tell me the truth or feed me more lies?

I towel myself dry and start to dress. There are fresh clothes at the end of the bed. It seems an absurd luxury given that I'd first dressed only two hours or so ago. I pull on the grey uniform but it isn't starched this time and the cotton sits soft against my skin. There's a knock at the door and a youngish Guardian enters, mid-twenties, I'd guess. Guardian 23. I haven't had any contact with her before. Her dark blue eyes match her uniform and they sparkle as she smiles. That confirms it – she hasn't been here long. The smiles usually go after a few months. I think of Guardian Rich. His smile lasted. Until it didn't. Smiles mean nothing.

'I've been asked to make you presentable,' she says with a grin, brandishing a hairbrush.

I say nothing. She sits on the bed and gestures for me to sit beside her.

'When's the last time you brushed this, then?' she says, laughing, but not unkindly, and I wince as she attacks yet another knot. She keeps going, tugging and pulling until my hair's left silky smooth and the roots smart. Finally, she ties it in a plait that hangs down my left shoulder and then looks at me quizzically.

'Now let's see about those eyes of yours. You haven't been getting your beauty sleep, have you, now.'

Out of a bag she produces a bottle of thick ivory cream and dabs little spots under my eyes, before rubbing them in, fingers working in gentle concentric circles.

'Much better,' she pronounces, holding up a little pocket mirror. The face staring back at me looks fresher, healthier, more relaxed. Only the eyes themselves remain suspicious, tense. They seem out of place. Like someone's made a poor choice in a collage.

Her satisfaction is short-lived, broken by a sharp exclamation.

'Oh … but your arms!'

My eyes follow the direction of hers to my upper arms. Greenish brown bruises are starting to form where Guardian 11 held me pinned. She dabs more ivory cream on them but it fails to work its magic this time and the bruises emerge like ghosts of their former selves. 'Here,' she says, rummaging inside her bag and producing a yellow scarf, 'wear this.'

I do as she says, wrapping the scarf over my upper arms like a shawl, a smile appearing on my lips despite myself. I think it's the colour. I've only ever worn grey before. Grey for seventeen years. So the yellow seems to radiate. It's like when you see the first dandelion on the grass. A beacon of summer.

'Now, if you sit here, I'll be back soon to take you to the library,' she says. 'The Supervisor said you're to meet the visitor there. I'll be no more than half an hour.'

I nod my acknowledgement and she leaves.

I sit and try to clear my head. To calm myself down. I know I'm going to need all my wits about me when the Mentor arrives so I should conserve my energy till then.

I try to concentrate on the sounds outside the room, on my breath, on the feel of the mattress against my legs and the floor against my feet.

But it doesn't work. I can't still my brain. It whirrs and questions. Ever since I told Guardian Rich about the geese it won't stop questioning.

If Guardian 23 only recently transferred here, where had she been before? Where were all the Guardians before? Were they in the Research City across the Wilderness? And if so, if there was room for more, why them, not us? They don't seem particularly special.

And then the same thought. The big one, returns.

Why are they so angry if I'm wrong about the Wilderness?

Followed by:

Why are they so angry if I'm right?

ARTHUR

Driving is freeing. The roar of the engine. The vibration of tyres on tarmac. The feeling of escape. The thought that you could go anywhere. Be anything. There's another car behind me, a silver sedan, but it's keeping its distance and I block it out.

I haven't been to Centre 6 before and the route is pleasanter than most. I leave the motorway and turn off onto a narrower road fringed by conifers. Opening the roof, I inhale the heady scent of pine. The conifers dwindle and then peter out as the road approaches the northernmost gate to the old nature reserve, to be replaced by shrub bushes and heathland. I glance in the rear-view mirror. The silver sedan is still there and it unnerves me. Who's trailing me and why?

Half a mile in and the landscape changes dramatically. It is barren, charred stumps arising from the blackened ground. My rational mind knows this is the result of controlled burning, to maintain the heathland habitat, but my reptile brain recoils at the apocalyptic sight of it all. A large caravan sits, apparently unoccupied, by the side of the road. I slow down as I pass it and see a sign on its side.

Stencilled in large capitals are the words – 'SILENCE. FILMING IN PROGRESS'.

The charred area is small and contained and I quickly leave it behind, trying to shed the uncomfortable feeling as a snake might its old skin. The road now cuts through swathes of short green grass with exposed sandy patches, embroidered with bundles of purple heather and flashes of yellow gorse. The strange feeling lingers though. I have never understood the appeal of this part of the country. There used to be ponies, of course, and a wild pony racing can lift the hardest of hearts, but now that they've been wiped out by a strain of equine flu, what else is there? Harsh remoteness that barely supports plant let alone animal life. It seems a fitting place to build a Centre.

My stomach twists and I can't tell how much is due to the landscape and how much is apprehension as to what will meet me ahead.

The road snakes left and the Centre comes into view. It's grander than the other three Centres I've been to. Sitting on slightly raised ground, it rises like a modern, grey castle from the land below, and I half expect to see a drawbridge and armoured knights atop battlements. I glimpse at the rear-view mirror. The sedan isn't following any more. It's parked some metres back. Someone going for a walk. Nothing more. I need to watch my paranoia.

There is no other building within sight for miles – only the Centre, the grass and the road and an overwhelming sense of loneliness.

Getting closer I see that, as usual, the Centre is surrounded by a high metal fence and the road just before it is blockaded by a barrier. There's an intercom to the right and I bring the car to a stop, lean out the window to press the buzzer and give my name. The barrier yawns open and I drive in. As with the other Centres, there is no entrance at ground level. Instead, the driveway immediately dips down and underground. I follow it and park in a basement bay.

Breathing deeply to calm my nerves, I get out the car and try to orient myself. Ahead is a brightly lit zone with 'Visitor's Entrance' written above a large steel door. I approach. There's a panel to the right of the door with a buzzer and a fingerprint sensor. I could let myself in, now I have updated security clearance for the whole of the building, but none the less I go to press the buzzer. A matter of courtesy as much as anything.

However, before I have a chance to actually touch the panel, the door swings open and a large woman appears, the strip lights throwing her exaggerated shadow at me. Tall, not overweight, but strong with a square jaw and hooded eyes that create a hawkish expression. The authority with which she walks and holds her considerable

131

frame leaves me in no doubt as to her identity. Ms Drake. The place's Supervisor.

She extends her hand towards me.

'Mr Easton. Welcome to Centre 6.'

ALBA

It's strange to be the only person in the library. It's never packed but there are normally at least a few tables full of people flicking through books, comparing pictures and facts. Apart from the volume of poetry I found that one time, it's only ever pictures and facts. I wish, really wish, that one day someone might write down a story – make something up, like Curly and I used to make stuff up to whisper to each other when we couldn't sleep.

OK, to be exact, I'm not the only person in the library now. Just the only student. Guardian 23 didn't fetch me from my room as promised. The far less friendly, bent-nosed Guardian 7 came instead and now he's standing just inside the library entrance, not even pretending to be interested in the books, but clearly there to guard against any possible escape on my part.

I try sitting at a table while I wait, but the apprehension just builds and builds until suddenly my knee's shaking, knocking against the underneath of the table and making it vibrate.

'I'm going to meet a Mentor,' my brain yells over and over again. 'I'm going to meet a Mentor. If anyone has answers, they will. Maybe they've even met Curly. Maybe they've got a message from her?'

I can feel my brain racing off into the world of fantasy.

I try pacing, but that doesn't work either. I need to distract myself. So I look at books. I go to try and find the *Chernobyl* book I looked at the other day, wanting to reassure myself that I didn't entirely make up the things about geese and feathers and oxidative stress. But it isn't there. The poetry book isn't there either on the shelf where I'd left it. I remember the place – between *Advanced Organic Chemistry 1* and *2*. I'd wanted to look at it again and those text books are so boring that I thought the chances of it being disturbed were basically nil.

The library and library corridor are both carpeted or I'd have heard their footsteps sooner. As it is, they steal up on me. The only advance notice is Guardian 7 suddenly snapping to attention and the door creaking open.

This is it.

The Mentor is here.

ARTHUR

The basement entrance is spotlessly clean, not a single footprint or speck of dust on the marble tiles. The lighting is warm and yellow and the walls are lined with calming photographs of landscapes and seascapes, the images filtered almost to abstraction. A vase of flowers sits on a console table against the wall and it is only when I brush my fingers against the leaves that I discern they are in fact silk. An imitation of life rather than life itself.

I follow the Supervisor down the corridor. There's a wood-panelled door on the left-hand side and I involuntarily flinch as we walk past, knowing what must lie behind.

At the end of the corridor I can see an entrance to a second unlit passageway off on the right, but I pay it no attention as the Supervisor has already called the lift, pressing her fingertip to the security panel.

The light goes from red to green, the doors close and we start to ascend.

I'm holding my breath as the lift doors open again. I don't even realise I'm doing it at first, only vaguely aware of a tightness in my throat and chest. We step out into a parquet corridor, the walls painted a neutral off-white. A couple of Hosts, aged twenty to twenty-five, I'd guess, clad in grey pressed uniforms walk past and try not to stare, their heads moving together to share whispered confidences once out of earshot.

'This way, Mr Easton.'

I don't know what I'd been expecting. A farm? A prison? Hosts grown in cages? The normality of it is both underwhelming and unnerving. The Supervisor pivots and begins marching left and I have to increase my normal walking speed to keep pace. We pass a number of glass-panelled doors that open off the corridor. Hosts are bent over books in one, doing yoga in another. All neatly presented. The boys, separate I note, also dressed in pale grey. They're not laughing but they don't look unhappy. In fact, it reminds me of my first school. Our uniform was grey and blue. Discipline was strict. But something jars. It is only when we reach the Supervisor's Office that I realise what it is. The walls. They are bare. No photos of the Hosts. No names on boards or plaques. No school motto. The whole place has the feel of a waiting room. A holding place.

I accept the Supervisor's offer of coffee out of knee-jerk politeness and watch her pour black liquid into a cup.

She attempts small talk. 'How was your journey?' 'Did you have any difficulty finding the Centre?' and I keep my answers brief, batting away the questions as one might flies at a picnic.

I remember reading somewhere that it takes a tenth of a second to form an impression of a stranger from their face and manner, fractionally longer to then process this impression into language. Impressions are based on the attractiveness, trustworthiness, likeability, competence and aggression of a person's features. I don't know whether it is her slight jowls, the tense set of her jaw, the frown lines on her forehead or the fact that her smile always takes slightly too long to form, like complicated clothes which, rarely worn, one has to work out how to wriggle into; in any event, my first impression of Ms Drake is of a deeply unpleasant woman, grown used to unfettered authority, whose attempts at charm are obsequious and repellent in equal measure.

She seems to think that I am here to audit the Centre and keeps apologising for the video. For its 'irregularity'. She says that she runs a 'very tight ship' here. That the Hosts' minds and bodies receive full exercise and scrutiny … and *care*. The last word she overemphasises as if to make up for the fact it was clearly added as an afterthought.

I place my cup down slightly too hard and it makes a clanging sound against the saucer.

'May I meet the girl now?' I ask in order to move matters along.

'The girl? You mean F3527? Of course. If you'll follow

me.' Her face struggles into its smile once again. 'F3527 is in the library. We make sure the Hosts have ample opportunity for self-improvement and relaxation.'

I follow her out of her office, down the main corridor and then left into a carpeted side corridor.

'Nearly there,' she says, injecting a false warmth into her voice.

The Supervisor pushes the door and it swings open.

And I see her for the first time.

She's sitting at a table in the middle of the room, holding a large hardback book. Her small frame is enveloped in a bright yellow scarf, a flash of gorse. Her hair is swept back off her face highlighting the pale luminosity of her skin. She turns to look at me, her eyes rising to meet mine. Intensely greeny-blue and flashing with a mix of fear, interest and defiance.

They pierce through the layers and I feel naked in front of her. Raw.

I was right.

She has eyes that see.

ALBA

He's not what I expected. Not what I expected at all. I'd been waiting for an old grey man, earnest and authoritarian. With glasses and a notebook. In the videos the Mentors, when they're not out in the Wilderness in hazchem suits, all wear glasses and are forever recording information in notebooks with serious expressions on their very erudite faces. But he's young. Around my age probably. How can someone my age be a Senior Mentor and Research Scientist? It makes no sense. But it's definitely him – the important visitor – he has power, I can see it. Feel it. From the way he stands. Occupies space as if he owns it. From the way the Supervisor stands that little bit away from him.

He's staring at me. Really staring. In a way I don't really understand. No one's stared at me like this before. And it's making me feel a weird mix of uncomfortable and important.

'You may leave us now.'

He speaks and the Supervisor obeys. I've never seen her take orders before. Her mouth opens as if to object and then closes, as if she thinks better of it, and she nods her agreement and stalks out the room. I smile and then he smiles too as if he caught it from me.

He has a nice smile. Wide, but not too toothy. Just the right amount of tooth, in fact, and no flash of gums. It always makes me feel a bit weird when people smile and you can see their gums. And even his smile seems genuine as it reaches his eyes. He has nice eyes – green with flecks of gold. His whole face seems to relax a bit with her out the room, as if someone's removed a plastic insert from it and it's fallen back into its natural form.

'May I?' he puts his hand on the top of the chair next to mine at the table and I nod, suddenly tongue-tied, as he pulls it out and sits down.

His knees are turned in so that they face mine and I think that's a bit of an invasion of body space until I look down and see that mine are turned in too. Knees just ten centimetres apart. Probably the closest I've ever been to a male other than Guardian Rich. I edge back, wary, then stop. I can't look like I want to get away. I want him to like me. Need him to like me. My survival depends on it.

'What are you reading?' he asks.

It takes me a moment to answer. His question catches me off guard. I was ready for an interrogation, an interview. Not questions. Normal conversational questions. It must be part of the test, I tell myself. To see if I'm someone they'd want to have around in the laboratory. They'd need some downtime in between all the science so it made sense to want someone who could engage in small talk.

'Um … a book about whales,' I stammer, then, trying to get my nerves under control, I show him a picture of a pod of humpback whales migrating. 'They're beautiful, don't you think?'

He nods. 'Very.' And he looks at me, as if searching my face for clues, I'm not sure what of.

'And clever,' I add. 'Did you know that whales can blow bubbles to create spiral-shaped fishing nets that trap fish and krill? It says here that people were amazed when they found this out. I think it's because whales are so huge that that's all people focused on before – their size – so they didn't expect them to be able to do anything else.'

What am I doing? I think. I'm trying to impress a Mentor and I'm jabbering on about whales. I press my lips together to stop any more words coming out and sit up straight, pulling back my shoulders at the same time, Curly's words in my ear. *Don't hunch. Don't ask too many questions.*

He smiles, tilting his head to one side like a robin from the *British Garden Birds* book. He doesn't look annoyed so I venture one further question. A question to get us back on topic.

'Do you think there're any left?' I ask. 'Whales, that is. Or do you think the radiation reached all the oceans too?'

He freezes momentarily, my mention of radiation seemingly touching a nerve, and that confirms it. He's not just a normal Mentor having a look around a Centre. He's here about the geese. He's seen my video interview and wants to find out what I know.

The silence suspends and drifts as he formulates an answer.

'Do you read a lot of books like this?' he asks.

And it's my turn to hesitate. He's sidestepping the question. Why does it matter what I read?

'I guess so,' I reply warily. 'Not always animals, some Chemistry and Physics too.'

'What about … novels?' he says.

I don't know what he's asking, what a 'novel' is. I could pretend I do and just say yes, I like them, but then what if novels are bad and the Creator disapproves and the right answer is 'I shun them and report anyone who has one'? It's too risky, so I go with the truth.

'I'm sorry, but I don't know what novels are,' I say quietly and register a flash of something that looks a bit like sadness pass across his face.

Panic rises. I'm failing the interview. I'm disappointing him and I can't afford to do that. I need him to pick me and to take me far, far away from here. He's the only reason the Supervisor has backed off. The reason I'm out of that horrible cell room. A little voice in the back of my brain adds *the only reason you're still alive.* I need him back on track. To impress him. There's only one thing to do. I need to be direct. I need to tell him what he's here to find out.

'Are you here about my interview?' I ask. 'About the geese?'

He gives me another of his mysterious looks and I still can't work out what he's feeling.

'In a way, yes,' he replies.

It's something, so I go with it.

'Shall I show you where I saw them?' I ask. 'Outside,' I add.

He gives himself a little shake and then replies, 'Yes. Yes, let's do that.'

Guardian 7 initially protests but soon backs down after a glare from the Mentor and I lead the Mentor back down the corridor and out through the side door, Guardian 7 remaining twenty paces behind.

It's cold outside and I have to pull the yellow scarf round me tightly to keep out the wind. We pass the barns and head towards the running track.

'This way…' I say and then I pause, realising I don't know if he actually is a Mentor or a Research Scientist or something altogether more important and in any event what the right way of addressing him is.

'Sorry,' I say. 'I don't know what I should call you. Should I say Mentor or Head Mentor or Sir?'

Another unreadable expression flits across his face before he answers.

'Arthur. You should call me Arthur.'

ARTHUR

I can't stop staring at her. It's like I'm a compass and she's due North. But I can see that she's afraid of me and I don't want to startle her so I ask her some mundane question about what she's reading. It surprised me after all. To see someone choose to read what looked like an encyclopaedia.

I don't know what I thought would happen if I met her. I think part of me hoped that I'd be blandly disappointed and that Tommy would be right. That I was projecting. Reading things into her that weren't there. That I'd find an averagely attractive creature with arresting eyes and that would be all. That I could then move on and transition in peace.

But as she starts talking about whales, I know that that's not really what I was hoping. That I wanted to be right.

And I am. There's an intelligence to her. A curiosity. And she talks guilelessly about the whales as if they were the most fascinating of creatures, completely unaware of her own hold over me.

Her question about the radiation catches me off guard and it takes a moment to settle myself. Of course. It makes complete sense. She thinks the same thing as the

145

Supervisor – that I'm here because of the geese, because of her deductions and the way they rip through the fabric of lies she's been fed. And in some way, I suppose I am.

I open my mouth to placate her with some line about the radiation, its spread or containment, but I find I can't do it. I'm sitting next to a girl who has been lied to her whole life and I can't add to that. Debate an imaginary Wilderness. I make myself a promise that I'll never lie to her. That I'll always tell her the truth.

Or freeze and sidestep the question like a coward.

I ask about novels. Because I genuinely want to know. I want to know why a girl who chose to recite a poem by Tennyson reads non-fiction books. Her answer cuts me like a knife. *What's a novel?* They're not allowed novels. I imagine how I would have survived the ordeal of losing Mother, of keeping Father, if I hadn't had the solace that stories provide, and I shudder. The Centre's policy makes logical sense, though. The Hosts are being raised as entities rather than humans. Numbered. Deferential to an all-seeing, all-knowing Creator. Exposure to novels or films would quickly cut through the deception they've been fed. It would show a world of human emotion and inspire them to dream. To question.

When she suggests we go outside it's like I've been given a lifeline and I clutch at it. The Guardian hovering at the door tries to object but quickly defers. I try to block out his presence behind us as we walk out of the building. I want it to be just the two of us.

She asks what she should call me and I tell her my name. I know she was looking for a title, a description, a number even, but I wanted her to have it. I'm pleased she asked. She repeats it, 'Ar-thur,' as if she's trying it on for size and I'm surprised by the pleasure it gives me just to hear my name upon her lips. She seems to savour the syllables, elongating them, giving the word a gravitas that was never there before. I want to be that sort of Arthur. Her Arthur. And that's how I want her to think of me. Not as Mr Easton. And certainly not as a Mentor.

Then a tiny crease appears in her forehead and she looks up at me, quizzically.

'What does it mean?'

I don't understand her question, so she repeats it.

'What does it, mean? "Arthur"? Names normally mean something.'

I think back to an early memory. I'm with Mother in our first proper house. She's curled up on the sofa, reading, and I'm standing next to her, clutching one of my first school reports, picking up the courage to show it to Father and face the inevitable tirade of disappointment. The report cover is red, scarlet even, and on the front in bold letters is printed Arthur Edward Easton. In that moment the name seems alien to me, foreign. A moniker belonging to someone else.

'How did you choose my name?' I asked Mother and she put down her book, looked at me, as in, really looked at me, and smiled. 'Your father chose it,' she replied. 'He was very insistent. Arthur is an ancient Celtic name meaning strong as a bear. Edward is an old English name meaning guardian of wealth.'

Father's choice made sense to me even then, as a little boy. Strength and money. Father's two priorities haven't changed much over the years.

I smile wryly to myself at the memory and then remember where I am and turn to face the girl. She's looking up at me with those same eyes that see and I feel like I'm trapped between worlds.

'Arthur means "strong as a bear",' I say.

'Oh,' she replies, interested. 'I've never heard that before.'

She looks at me differently after I've told her my name. She's still wary, I can see that, but there's a lightness there too that wasn't there before, an inner light that turns her eyes into glowing greeny-blue orbs. I feel the wonder that an astronaut must when gazing at the world from space. Finally, a smile spreads over her lips. A perfect, slightly lopsided smile. Spontaneous rather than conjured.

'I'm F3527,' she says and then hesitates, as if uncertain whether to continue. '…But my best friend calls me Alba, after alabaster. Because of my skin.'

Surprise raises my eyebrow and creases my brow. She has a name? They name themselves? I feel like I've been winded and it takes me a minute to register that her face has become a mask of horror and fear and she's twisting on her ankles as if preparing to flee.

'I'm sorry. I'm so sorry,' she begs, hands intertwined, pulling at the fingers, knuckles becoming rosaries. 'Please forget I said that. And don't tell the Supervisor, will you? Please don't tell her. We're not supposed to have names.'

Guilt pierces me and I rush to reassure her.

'No, no, you haven't done anything wrong. I'm so glad you told me,' I stumble over the words as they rush out of my mouth, desperate to appease her. 'It's a beautiful name,' I say. 'Pleased to meet you, Alba.' I smile and then finally she smiles back at me and it's like we've made a secret pact, sharing names instead of blood.

She takes me down to the running track to point out the exact place that she saw the geese. I point to the ground to show my interest and then she takes my hand and adjusts it slightly to the right. Her hand is soft and fragile inside my own, like a bird skeleton, but it's not cold. It's warm. Pulsing with energy, with life. I wrap my fingers over hers. Encasing them.

She looks up at me and asks in a small voice, 'Do you believe me? About all of it?'

'I do,' I reply and she smiles again and all I can think is

that I want to make this girl smile that way at me for the rest of my life.

'Will I see you again?' she asks.

'Yes,' I reply firmly. 'I'll come back tomorrow.' My words take me by surprise. Their certainty. Tomorrow. But there are no other options. I have to see her again and tomorrow is already too far away. 'Can I…' I hesitate. 'Can I bring you anything?'

Her brow furrows in concentration and she pivots again on her ankles as she thinks.

'Can you bring me a novel? I'd like to see what a novel is.'

'A novel it is,' I reply.

I realise I'm still holding her hand and she's made no move to pull it away. We're standing here, silently, both looking at her hand in mine and for the first time in years I feel like I'm home.

A bell rings, ripping me from my reverie and I become aware of the shadowy silhouette of the Supervisor behind me, a not-so-subtle indicator that I have already outstayed my welcome.

I leave her outside. Alba. Turning once to look back as I walk away, I see the Guardian, next to her now, hand roughly circling her arm. I ball my hand into a fist. He'd better not hurt her. I'll have his job if he hurts her.

ALBA

I watch him walk away, an invisible thread lengthening between us like a skein of wool unravelling, wishing all the time that I could tug at it and pull him back. The wind is picking up, nipping at my cheeks and it's like I can taste the air. Hints of recently cut grass and cabbage leaf and tarmac.

I can't believe that I did that, held his hand like that. Some people are really touchy-feely. Always putting their hand on your arm to make a point when they're telling you something. Rusty, who got picked a couple of months back, used to slap you on the back whenever she made a joke. I'm not like that. I'm not a back slapper or hand holder. And I don't think even Rusty would have grabbed the hand of a super-important visitor from the City.

I never would have done it if he hadn't told me his name. If I hadn't told him mine. Arthur and Alba. Alba and Arthur. It's like by reciting them we'd made a spell that had broken all the normal rules.

The only other hand I've held is Curly's, but that was different. That was comfort. Safety. This wasn't. This was electricity. A tiny charge sitting in my palm, pulsing, like the drawings you see in books about Van de Graaf generators. Is it because he was a male? Is this why we can't have lessons with the males? I shake my head even though there's no one other than myself here to convince. I haven't held any of the males' hands before but I've walked next to them down the corridors. Sat near them in assembly. There was never anything passing between us like this. No spark. It wasn't even the way he looked, really. He looked nice, obviously. But it was more than that. It was something about him. Something inside. His questions. His interest.

And he believes me. About the Wilderness. I could see it in his eyes and not in that hooded predatory 'now I think you're dangerous and I'm going to destroy you' way the Supervisor had.

I think he knows what's going on.

And I think he's going to tell me.

I don't get to think any longer. Suddenly Guardian 7's by my side, his right hand wrapped round my upper arm in a vice-like grip. It hurts. He squeezes further, just for kicks, and tears prick at the corners of my eyes. Furiously, I blink them away. I'm not going to let him see me cry.

'Come on,' he says, gruffly. I'm to go back to my room. My cell. My hope, the little kernel of joy that meeting Arthur had brought, starts to wither, ground to paste. I'm not safe. I'm here. At the mercy of the Supervisor and a visitor that, let's face it, I hardly know. He might change his mind. People do. He might keep walking and never come back. I can't help it. The tears start to fall now. Fall properly. And I don't even care that Guardian 7 sees.

But then it happens. Arthur stops. Just momentarily. But he stops on the path a few steps before he reaches the side door. Stops and looks back. At me.

And I feel like my heart might burst.

ARTHUR

The Supervisor waits until we are back inside her office before interrogating me.

'So?' she asks, trying to make her voice sound friendly and failing.

'Yes?' I answer curtly. I'm in no mood to deal with her now. I want to think about Alba. The feel of her hand in mine. The pulse under her skin. About the way she looked at me. The way she makes me feel like I'm floating, high above the earth.

'Was F3527 to your liking?'

I wince at the F3527. She's not F3527. She's a girl. Alba.

The Supervisor mistakes my expression for displeasure and starts speaking faster.

'The Host is small, granted, but she has been fully screened and is in perfect health. She shows no particular genetic susceptibility to heart disease, cancer or arthritis.' The Supervisor lowers her voice and leans in. I can smell the milky coffee residue on her breath. It has a bitter, stale sweetness. I lean back but she just leans in further and continues regardless. 'And like all the female Hosts here, the Host is ... intact.' Her attempts at delicacy don't suit her.

I'm beginning to feel claustrophobic, the walls of her office closing in on me. I say nothing and concentrate on my breathing. I try to imagine I'm not here. I'm outside, back in the fresh air again. Alba's hand in mine.

The Supervisor's still talking but her voice sounds far away now. I'm slowly managing to tune it out. I can only just make out the next words.

'Which brings us to more practical issues … will you be reserving her?'

Reserving. Her.

I'm back on the ground with a thump, hearing restored, heart racing. I remember why I'm here. What people like me do.

She takes my silence for disinterest.

'Because if not, we should push ahead with emergency transition. Having watched the video. I'm sure you understand that. She cannot remain here. The potential damage that will result if she shares her ideas amongst the other Hosts is simply too great.'

Emergency transition.

Never.

I can't lose her. I've only just found her.

'No, no. I wish to reserve her.'

There's a strange buzzing in my ear and it's getting louder.

'And what date should I put?'

No words come. My head won't engage.

'The maximum length of reservation is three days. Which would take us to this Friday.'

'Right.'

I've got a headache now. I can tell it's going to be a bad one.

'Shall I put down Friday 22nd then?'

'Yes.'

My vision is beginning to pixelate. I need to lie in the dark.

'Very good, sir.'

'And I'll be back tomorrow.'

She stares at me, one eyebrow raised.

'11am,' I continue. I want it timetabled, official. A prearranged time seems to make it official.

'…Very good, sir.'

I stagger back to the car and take two of the green pills Tommy gave me. And close my eyes.

Half an hour later I'm on the road again.

I glance in the rear-view mirror.

The silver sedan is back.

ALBA

Forty-nine, fifty.

I collapse back on the floor. Sweat pooling on my forehead and in the small of my back. Exercise helps. The pain in my abs from the second round of sit-ups is a welcome distraction. If my brain can focus on the burn, it has less time to whirr and panic.

Otherwise I'm going to go mad in here.

I close my eyes and picture the sky. White plumes of clouds painted on the blue. Then it's no longer the sky. It's Arthur's face. He's smiling at me. And he's saying he'll take me away.

Far, far away.

On the way back inside we'd passed Guardian 11 wheeling in the trolley with this week's food delivery. A thought that I hadn't even realised had been nagging away at my head suddenly exploded out of my mouth.

'The food?' I asked Guardian 7 as the trolley turned the corner. 'Does that come in some sort of hazmat suit?'

'What? … no … what are you talking about?' He twisted my arm tighter from annoyance.

And I felt my stomach drop even more. The geese cross

the Wilderness and they're fine. The food crosses the Wilderness and it's fine.

I wasn't right. The Wilderness isn't lifting. It's lifted.

They know it. They all know it.

So why the hell are we still here?

I lie my head back and then start a third round of sit-ups.

One, two, three…

ARTHUR

I'm late for golf with Tommy.

I tried to cancel but he wasn't answering his phone. Clubhouse rules are that phone calls are not to be taken inside the grounds. They're probably the only rules Tommy actually obeys.

When I arrive, he's waiting at the first tee, immaculately turned out in navy tweed plus fours and an argyle knitted vest. I think he prefers the clothes to the game. He taps his watch in exaggerated annoyance as I approach.

'I'm not used to being stood up, you know?' he drawls, while making a show of selecting the right club. 'I'm the stander-upper … not the stander-upee.' He pulls out his newest fairway wood, chuckling at his own wit before fixing me with a devilish grin.

I'm expected to join in, I know I am, but I can't summon anything resembling the facsimile of a smile. Instead I mumble an excuse and feel his eyes hot on me, scanning me, my body language, my facial expressions.

He lets out a low, slow whistle.

'You were with her, weren't you?'

My heart rate quickens. I shouldn't have told Tommy I

was going to meet her. I'm not ready to talk about it yet. About her yet. I should have gone straight home and slept.

'So how was she?'

I rifle through my clubs. It's a short hole. A wood would be overkill. I know I'm not fooling Tommy – I've never cared for golf. A pointless game. A futile way to pass a futile existence. But I need to buy myself some time.

'Arthur?' His voice is gentle. This time he's not goading me. He's genuinely concerned.

'Yes, all right, I met her.' And then suddenly, out of nowhere, the need to share overwhelms me.

'I was right, Tommy. She's amazing. She's not like a machine at all. She's clever and curious. She absorbs information like a sponge. She knew all these facts about whales!'

Tommy's saying nothing, just staring at me strangely and I feel this heat spread up my back. I just keep talking to fill the void.

'They give each other names, did you know that? She's Alba. *Alba*. Like Alabaster. Because her skin's so pale.'

Tommy puts down his golf club.

'But they don't let them read books. Novels, that is.'

Tommy still isn't saying anything.

There's a loud 'tut' from behind us as an impatient group of golfers standing at the edge of the fairway wait their turn to tee off.

160

Tommy rounds on them, raising his voice.

'Do you know who this is? Arthur Easton, son of Michael Easton, heir to the M.A.D.E. corporation?' The tuts stop and the faces register a new emotion instead. Fear. Level Ones, all of them. Always aware who granted them their longevity and who could decide to take it all away.

'So sorry. Please take your time,' the sandy-haired one stutters.

'We'll come back later,' the ginger-haired one adds before they back away, heads lowered. I want to sink into the ground.

'Don't worry about them, Artie.'

Artie.

Tommy hasn't called me that since we were eight. He waits until the other golfers are out of earshot.

'What's going on? You were supposed to see if you wanted to *become* her. Not fall for her.'

'I'm not falling for her,' I snap. But my anger is exaggerated. He's hit a nerve. Deep down I know this isn't just intellectual curiosity. I am no longer searching for an echo of my mother. I am falling for her. Falling for a Host that I hardly know and whom I am scheduled to download into in three days' time.

'If you don't choose her, someone else will,' Tommy says, as if reading my mind. 'At least this way you get to look at her in the mirror.'

'Stop. Stop talking.' My voice is raised. I'm sweating.

'Oh, Artie,' Tommy says and then wraps his arms around me and holds me tight. 'Let's forget the golf and go and get truly shit-faced somewhere.'

ALBA

In the dorms the Guardians used to knock before they came in. They'd have entered anyway and they often already had the door slightly ajar before the 'knock' sounded, but it was a small nod towards respecting our privacy. The acknowledgement that we might merit it. Here, by myself, there's no pretence at privacy, the arrival of a Guardian announced by the sound of a key, turning in the lock. I look up. It's Guardian 17. Instinctively I tense up. She's looking at me with an expression I can't quite place and carrying paper and a pen. She places them both on a desk in the corner and then re-tucks her hair behind her ears. I walk over to her, trying to gauge what she wants. Every interaction is now a game. An opportunity to find out what's really going on.

She glances over her shoulder before speaking. As it's just the two of us in the room it seems unnecessary, pointless.

'How was it – the meeting?' she asks, in a quiet, almost needy voice, as if afraid we might be overheard.

The Creator sees everything. The Creator hears everything.

I realise I've thought a lot less about the Creator these past few days.

'The visitor,' she prompts. 'What was he like?' There's a wide-eyed curiosity to her. She's hungry for information. And it gives me an unexpectedly warm glow inside. I've met someone special. I know it. And others seem to know it too.

'Fine,' I say and shrug, suppressing a smile. I'm not sharing. I'm keeping him all to myself.

'Suit yourself,' she snaps and points to the papers laid out on the desk.

The sheet on the left is filled with handwriting. The writing is in fountain pen – I can tell by the colour of the ink and the way it seems to seep into the paper – the letters large and looping and slanting to the right, as if in a hurry to make their mark on the page. On the right is a pile of paper, empty, demanding to be filled. I touch a piece. It is thick and textured, quite unlike the paper we normally use.

I can't help myself. Despite everything, a smile forms on my lips. It's the same! It's the same task Curly was set when she was chosen, although she had to use a normal biro and the writing she copied was nothing like as beautiful as this. It confirms it. Arthur wants me. He's chosen me. I'm going to be his Apprentice. I'm going to leave this place and there's nothing the Supervisor can do to stop it. I can worry about the rest of it later.

'You're to copy out the handwriting, matching the style as accurately as possible. Copy each line at least fifty times. I'll be back later to check on your progress.'

She leaves the room abruptly and I sit down at the desk and pick up the pen, cradling it between my thumb and middle finger. It feels heavy in my hand. We usually write with biros rather than fountain pens. The pen's body is a distinguished navy blue and the nib gleams silver when it catches the light from the window. Just holding it makes me feel important. I never want to write with anything else again.

I copy the first line.

'The results are inconclusive and should be repeated.'

I stare at the result. The loops are wrong and the capital 'T' lacks the curved flourish of the original. My hand hurts from the movement. Tiny muscles it doesn't usually engage being worked and stretched. The finger equivalent of three rounds of sit-ups.

I try again and again and smile. The loops are better. The T's still terrible, the flourish like some sort of weird lightning bolt, but still – I'm improving.

I don't know why they get us to do this. They must be very particular about the way you write in the Research City. Want everyone in the group they join to write the same.

'The results are inconclusive and should be repeated.'

Still not there. My hand is cramping but I ignore it. I finish the fifty and move on to the second line.

'I suggest a larger sample size.'

I'm going to be the best Apprentice they've ever had.

ARTHUR

We're back at Tommy's as he said I shouldn't be at mine tonight. That I'd brood too much. He's fixed me a drink and left me on his sofa while he rummages round at the back of a cupboard off his spare bedroom to 'get something', exactly what the 'something' is, omitted in a deliberate attempt to provoke me. It failed. I'm too tired to be annoyed.

'Have you found it yet?' I call. I came here for company, for distraction, after all, and Tommy has been gone for over ten minutes.

'Not it, them!' comes the triumphant reply and Tommy re-emerges carrying two face masks, something thin and translucent draped over his left wrist.

Tommy follows my stare.

'Latex gloves,' he says.

Of course.

'I'm taking you out-out. We don't want to bump into Davina, Freddie, Daisy and that lot. So we're going to a DMW joint. And we need to blend in.'

I try to protest but Tommy's having none of it. 'It'll do you good. Doctor's orders. We'll have a few drinks.

Dance. You can leave when you want to. Scout's honour.'
He touches three fingers to his forehead in a mock
salute.

If I'm honest, the idea excites me. I haven't been out for
ages. Nights with Tommy's crowd no longer interest me.
All polish, no substance. Dry conversations and recycled
wit. But a DMW joint? I thought most had closed. Trust
Tommy to have found out one that's still going.

There is something intoxicating about the idea of being
someone else for a night. Someone who people don't shy
away from. Someone who isn't Michael Easton's son.

The night air is cold and I pull my coat tightly round
me, pulling up the collar to protect my neck from the
sharp breeze. Mask and gloves on, I already feel freer. We
board a bus – *if we're going to do this, let's do it right. DMW
from start to finish* – Tommy's words, not mine, and head
to the east end. I never come to this end of town so I have
no markers, nothing to recognise and navigate by and I'm
entirely dependent on Tommy for directions. Tommy
confidently heads down a dark side road and then down
an even more suspect-looking alleyway on the right. The
houses on either side rise up, dark and decaying, their
entrances shrouded in shadow. I hear the regular pat of
footsteps behind us, the speed matching our own. I glance
behind us but there's no one there.

'Are you sure you know where you're going?' I ask.

Tommy smiles in reply, pointing towards a sign I hadn't spotted hanging from a building further up on the right.

DMD. The letters are painted in gold against a black backdrop.

I raise an eyebrow.

'Dead Men Dancing,' Tommy grins appreciatively. 'Can't say they don't have a sense of humour.'

We draw level with the sign and see that it hangs over steps that curl down to a basement door. The bouncer on the door is huge, arms the size of my thighs, neck barely present. The face mask makes him even more threatening. He looks us up and down for obvious signs of infection – blood flecks on the masks, open sores and the like and then lifts the rope. We're in.

The music is insanely loud. Tommy tries to say something to me, but I can't hear it. All the cells in my body start vibrating and, like everyone else in there, I just start dancing. There's a wildness to the place. Like everyone is here because they need to be. Need to be around other people. Need the company of strangers just for one night. Just to feel less alone.

When dancing used to be more of a thing, I was a timid dancer. Arms to the side, legs barely moving, relieved when the slow numbers came on as you knew what was expected of you. But here; here you had to really dance. To let your arms and legs and body go crazy. One with the rhythm. It was nothing like the music that our usual crowd listen to. No drawn-out notes. No one crooning into the mic. Instead, the rhythm mirrors my pulse. Only faster. More intense. A collective heartbeat joining each and every one of us.

A guy to my right with a shock of thick black hair catches my eye and smiles. Well, I think he does. I can't see his mouth, but his eyes crinkle up and shine. I smile back. It's not flirtatious, it's an acknowledgment. We're both here. Alive. Tonight.

The rotating mirrorballs above our heads catch the light and diffract it, spinning rainbow shards across the ceiling. Shards that scatter, fragment and reform.

Tommy's off somewhere but I'm fine with that. I'm not here to talk. I'm here to lose myself. All sensations are alien. The cloth of the face mask against my lips and nose as I breathe. The feeling of latex on my fingers. The way my hands shimmer slightly if I hold them up to the lights.

I glance to my right. A couple are dancing together. One body so perfectly fitting the other that it's as if they've been chiselled from the same block of stone. The music shifts slightly and it's as if it's a cue as they both lower their masks at the exact same time and start kissing. Mouths locked, tongues burrowing, fingers tracing muscles. I'm stunned slightly, shocked by the risks that they are taking, and I see the black-haired guy look similarly amazed. But it makes sense, I guess. Contact. Love. The most human of all emotions. Staring at them I think of Alba and imagine kissing her. How soft her mouth would be. The feeling of her lips against mine.

I'm so caught up in my thoughts that it dulls my senses and it takes me a moment to notice that the girl to my left has stopped flailing around to the music and has started coughing. Really coughing. The coughs rack her body so she's bent over double and her chest is heaving and heaving. The black-haired guy stops dancing too. The girl stands up and her face mask is tinged red. Like a clown's mouth has been painted on it. It takes me a moment to register what's going on. I'm not prepared. This isn't my world.

'Help me!' she mumbles, the mask muffling her words. No one moves.

She rips the mask off to reveal blood-flecked spittle foaming at the edges of her mouth.

Everything goes into slow motion. The couple to my right pull their masks back on in horror and back away. I move in the girl's direction to help her, but the black-haired guy moves forward to grab me.

'Are you insane?' he yells.

The music stops. Someone in charge has noticed what's going on. The girl's still coughing, pink drops of saliva landing on the floor, on clothes, on skin. Everyone panics, wide-eyed, trampling over one another in a rush to get out of the place.

I'm frozen. Frozen to the spot. Just staring at the girl. Watching the horror on her face and not knowing how to help. This is what it's like, I realise. If you don't have regular testing, if you can't transition, this is what it's like. One moment you're dancing, you don't even know you're infected. The next you're coughing blood. Or you're inhaling someone else's blood and that's it. Your existence is over. Erased before you've made your mark. Before anyone's even realised you're there.

An arm snakes behind me and pulls me away and up the steps.

The outside air seems so fresh it almost stings my lungs. Everyone's standing around, laughing. Laughing with an edge of mania. Someone's started a small fire in the middle of the alley and people are peeling off blood-specked clothes and feeding them to the flames. Tommy spots me and comes over, as does the Asian guy.

'Thanks,' I say.

'For what?' Tommy replies, smiling.

'For getting me out of there. I don't know what happened to me.'

'Wasn't me, old chap,' Tommy laughs.

I turn to the black-haired guy.

'Not me either,' he gets in before I have a chance to

thank him instead. 'Seems you have a guardian angel…
Good thing, really.'

'Your friend's got a suicide wish,' the black-haired guy
confides to Tommy after I introduce them. 'What were
you thinking, man, going to touch her like that? You'll get
yourself killed.' He shakes his head and then leans in
towards me. 'We're not Level One bastards, you know?'

Guilt hits me like a freight train and my head's reeling.

'I see them here sometimes,' he continues, oblivious.
'Like they're so daring. Like they're dancing with death.'
He spits at the ground. 'Frickin poverty tourists.'

I start to sway.

*We don't die like they do. Like she does. Alba… I'm sorry,
I'm so sorry.*

Tommy catches me before I hit the floor.

ALBA

I wake in the middle of the night from a horrific dream. I was in this same room but the door was open. I wandered into the corridor but no one was there. I went to the main bit of the building and then the dining hall and the library. The same. I was the only one left. All the other students, the Guardians, the Supervisor had gone. And I was here, all alone. I went outside and from the top of the mound I could see a series of figures walking away down the road that leads away from the Home. I could make out the back of Curly and Arthur's heads. They were holding hands. I screamed at them but they couldn't hear me. I screamed again but they kept walking until they were just specks on the horizon. Then they were gone.

Breathless, I switch on the light. The clock reads 3am. I know I'm not going to get back to sleep so I pull the quilt round my shoulders for warmth and go and sit at the desk. In front of me lie the pages of handwriting. I put my finger out and trace the curling loops of the original page. The touch, skin to ink, calms me. It's proof I tell myself. Proof I'm getting out of here.

ARTHUR

I'm exhausted but on edge, so sleep eludes me. Tommy brought me back home but I managed to convince him to leave and let me rest. I told him I was exhausted, nothing more.

'It's the tumour,' Tommy insisted. 'Transition. Get it done.'

I smiled at him as if I were considering it as I showed him to the door.

I consider fixing myself a brandy to steady my nerves but decide against it. I've already had too much to drink and I don't want a hangover tomorrow. Nothing to dull my time with Alba. Instead I make myself a coffee and comb through the bookshelves that line the far end of the living room. I promised her a novel. What would be the perfect first book? It should be a classic, I decide. Something that's stood the test of time and speaks to generations, to the human condition. To pretend she is anything else is absurd. *Jane Eyre? Great Expectations?* Then it jumps out at me. Third shelf from the top. *Moby Dick.* It's a First Edition. A gift from Father on finishing my Middle School exams. To 'help you become a man' reads the inscription inside. The implication being that I wasn't one already; that then, as now, there was always room for improvement. The cover is dusty and slightly torn and I haven't looked at it for years. But it's perfect. It'll make her smile. Her perfect, lopsided grin.

I take my fountain pen and open the book to the title page. With a decisive line, I strike through Father's words and substitute my own beneath. I feel a frisson of excitement, as if by eliminating his words I am to some extent eliminating his influence over my life.

For Alba, I write.

Who recognises that whales are more than massive.

Love,

Arthur.

I hadn't intended to write the 'love'. The word appears on the page as if by will of the pen or force of habit rather than by my hand. But seeing it there pleases me.

I laugh wryly. Father would be horrified. Defiling a rare First Edition to give it to a Host. He'd see it as proof that his son had finally lost his mind.

ALBA

Guardian 8 tells me that Arthur's coming at 11 when he delivers my breakfast tray of porridge topped with nuts and cream instead of the normal raisins.

'Eat it all,' he says as he put it on the desk. 'Supervisor's orders. You've lost too much weight.'

I try to eat. Pick up the spoon and force in mouthful after mouthful, but my stomach knots and tightens and I have to stop.

I get myself dressed in another freshly laundered and pressed tunic and brush my hair but it won't sit right. It lies flat on top and then curls up a bit on the right-hand side. I try tying it up but that draws attention to the dark smudges under my eyes and the hollows that have started forming in my cheeks. I keep hoping that Guardian 23 will be back with more of her miracle cream but she isn't. Maybe they think that now he's chosen me they don't need to work so hard. But he can still change his mind, can't he?

Shush brain, I tell myself. He clearly didn't choose you for your looks. There are far prettier girls here.

At ten to eleven the door opens and Guardian 17

enters. 'Come on,' she says brusquely as if I've been dawdling rather than sitting, captive in my room. 'We don't want to be late.'

I follow her down the winding corridors, trotting to keep pace with her longer strides. When we reach the main corridor, she doesn't turn left towards the library as I'd been expecting. She turns right instead, finally stopping outside the Supervisor's Office. My heart sinks and my windpipe constricts. Why were we here? Has Arthur lost interest already and left me for the Supervisor to get rid of? But then why does she want to feed me up? It makes no sense.

Guardian 17 raps at the door and we're called inside. I follow behind Guardian 17, mirroring her movements, as if her body would somehow act as a shield.

'She's ready for you,' pipes up the Supervisor's assistant in her reedy voice, so we head straight through the second set of doors and into the Supervisor's Office.

I look down at the carpet and then risk an upwards glance. The Supervisor's risen from behind her desk and she's staring at me, fixing me with her snake eyes. But something seems wrong with her face. Her mouth doesn't match her eyes. It's ... smiling. Well, the corners are turned up anyway as if accidentally glued to her cheekbones, revealing all her top teeth. It reminds me of the book about chimpanzees in the library. When chimpanzees 'smile' with their top teeth it's actually a threatening expression designed to intimidate. A declaration of war. When I read it I didn't get how a smile could be intimidating. Now I do. I force myself not to flinch as I try to make sense of the situation.

Then a movement to my right catches my eye and I turn to see him, Arthur, sitting in the leather armchair in the corner by the window. He's leaning forwards, smiling too. But his isn't a weird, disturbing grimace. It's a smile with genuine warmth. Directed at me. He hasn't gone. He's here and he's pleased to see me. Really pleased. My anxiety thaws and I beam back, wishing again that I'd been able to make myself prettier this morning. That said, looking closer, he looks tired too. Something about the way he's not sitting totally straight and there – around his eyes – there's a bluish tinge that matches my own. It's always eyes that are the giveaway. And his eyes, although they twinkle, are tinged with sadness. I have a sudden urge to reach out and stroke the blue away with my thumb. Gently erase it. And then to cradle his head in my arms and tell him that everything is going to be all right. I don't, of course. I'm not an idiot.

'I thought it would be best for you to meet in here today,' the Supervisor says. Her voice is unnecessarily loud for the size of the room and reverberates off the walls. 'Your walk-about yesterday caused a bit too much excitement amongst the students.' She tries to speak with a lightness to her tone, but it's obvious she doesn't find anything amusing about what she's saying.

Here. Talk to him *here*. In *her* office. The words thump in my head and the anxiety's back. I can't talk to Arthur here. In front of her.

Arthur stands, drawing himself up to full height. He's about five centimetres taller than the Supervisor and it's clear he's trying to make each one of them count.

'Thank you for vacating your office for us,' he says. 'Most kind of you.'

The Supervisor opens and closes her mouth and I stifle a laugh which is bubbling up inside. It's clear she had no intention whatsoever of going anywhere and now she's left with the option of either leaving, tail between her legs, or facing down a very important Mentor.

'Of course,' she finally manages to say. 'I shall return in an hour.'

He won. He actually won. He's stronger than her. Arthur's power seems dizzying, intoxicating.

An hour, however, is no time at all. I wait for him to tell her it has to be two hours, or three or four. But he doesn't. It's like all the fight he had in him has been used up. Instead, he nods his agreement and the deal is struck.

I stand, shifting awkwardly from foot to foot, not quite sure what to do with myself, not quite sure what is expected of me. Arthur jumps up and, apologising profusely, looks around for a chair for me to sit on. There are none apart from the Supervisor's so he goes behind her desk and pulls it out for me and I perch on the front, edging away from the back as if it were radioactive. Even with the Supervisor out of the room it takes me a while to relax in there, sitting on that. Associations are powerful things, I guess. I look at Arthur and suddenly I'm tongue-tied. It's like I've got so much to say, to ask, but no idea how to put it into words. He's looking at me, concerned, and I'm worried he's misremembered me and is now disappointed as I don't live up to the idea of me that he'd built up in his head. But I still can't think of anything to say.

The ticking of the clock on the mantelpiece is almost unbearably loud. Tick. Tick. Tick.

'Tea?' he asks, nodding towards a fancy teapot and cups set out on a tray. I nod, gratefully, glad to have something to do. A prop to hold.

'You look tired,' he says passing me the cup and saucer. Our fingers brush as I take it and there it is again – that same spark, the flash of electricity that I felt before. My hand trembles, sending the cup clattering against the saucer and I quickly put them down, embarrassed. I feel my cheeks burning with shame but he doesn't laugh at me. Instead, with trembling fingers of his own, he leans in and traces the skin under my eyes.

'I didn't sleep well,' I confess.

'Me neither,' he says with his sad grin again.

Then, suddenly, he darts away and begins rifling around in the bag that's lying by his feet. He pulls out what looks like a really old thick book.

'I promised you a novel, didn't I?' His head is slightly tilted to one side and his face is alight with anticipation, left eyebrow raised like a question mark. *Did I do well?*

I take it gingerly – it's heavy and I don't want to drop it – and I stare in wonder at the book in my hands. The cover is a faded light brown, peeling in places, with the title embossed in gold on the spine. I hold it up to the window to see the lettering more clearly. *Moby Dick or The Whale* by Herman Melville. I smile, staring up at him in wonder. He'd listened. He'd heard me talk about whales and remembered. I can't wait to go to the Research City with him and spend every minute of every day with this man. I open the book and feel the pages, flicking through them with my thumb. They are thin and yellowish with a strange smell, a bit like the patch of yellow plaster at the back of the showers or the spare blankets we fetch from the storage room on particularly cold winter nights. I put my nose to the paper and inhale and then suddenly there's this tickle in my nose and it's rising and then I'm sneezing. Sneezing uncontrollably over this novel, spraying droplets everywhere.

'Noooo!' a silent scream builds in my throat. 'Noooooo! What have I done!' The Seventh Commandment. Do not sneeze. If you sneeze it must be into a clean tissue which is then incinerated.

'I'm so sorry, I'm so sorry,' I whisper. 'But I'm not ill, I promise. Not even a cold. Please don't tell her.' My eyes sweep the ceiling, looking for cameras, anything that could be recording us, collecting evidence.

'Don't worry,' he says. His voice sounds, strange. 'Please don't worry,' he laughs. I can't believe he's laughing. 'It's the dust. I should have warned you.'

My heart rate starts to return to normal. It's the dust. Just the dust. 'Do all novels make you sneeze?' I ask.

Again, he seems to find me amusing. 'Only the old ones. It's a First Edition. One of the first copies of this book ever printed.'

Then he glances down before meeting my eyes again. Something's changed. He's not laughing any more. He almost seems … shy.

'Here, it's yours now.'

He opens the book a couple of pages in. The words haven't started yet, just the title printed again in the middle of the page. At the top of the page there's some handwriting with a line crossed through it, but that's not what first draws my eye. It's the bottom of the page. The handwritten words that lie there.

For Alba.

Who recognises that whales are more than massive.

Love,

Arthur.

Different thoughts and emotions compete for attention and jostle their way to the surface.

Love, Arthur.

I can't help but wonder what it means. It's not like I'd never heard the word before. The Supervisor loves order. Guardian 17 loves freshly picked carrots. Guardian Rich loves rainbows. I love Curly and she loves me.

But Arthur doesn't know me. How could he think I was one of his favourite things? How could he *love* me?

Do I love him?

I like him. I think I like him a lot. And I already trust him more than anyone here. I've looked forward to seeing him all morning with his smile and his concern and his golden eyes. And I want him to sit next to me and look at me and my heart's beating faster as I think he might be about to hold my hand again. Is that love?

I force myself to focus on something else. Anything else.

The handwriting. I know the handwriting. I'd recognise it anywhere – after all, I've stared at nothing else for most of the night. The loops, the swirls, the way it chases to the right. The flourish of the capital A. It's his handwriting

183

I've been copying. A smile dances on my lips. They are definitely preparing me to work for him.

Then suddenly, out of nowhere, tears of emotion are pricking at the edge of my eyes. Furiously I blink them away and look for something else to distract me. I begin to read the inscription above. The one that's been crossed out.

For Arthur,

May this book help you become a man.

Your Father.

I frown in confusion.

'What's a "father" I ask?'

ARTHUR

What have I done? What the hell have I done? She's staring at me. Staring with those intense bluey-green eyes of hers. Searing through the layers of skin, muscle, bone, to my very soul, if indeed I have one left, looking for answers. Tommy said to be careful. That they have been fed this elaborate fiction. It gives them comfort, happiness. An integral system with its own rules and own sense of coherency. They don't know about families. Fathers, mothers. You can't miss or mourn the absence of something you don't know even exists. And to introduce something alien – to question the omniscience of the Creator – to introduce doubt is to act like the serpent in Eden – their whole reality crumbles, comes falling down like a house of cards.

I desperately try to think of something to say to make everything better, to placate her but I can't think of anything and the longer I'm silent the wider her eyes become and the deeper runs the crease between her eyebrows. I should have thought before I gave her the book. She's curious, intelligent. I should have known she'd read Father's inscription and that the word would jump out at her. I wanted to make her happy. To show her that I cared. But it was selfish. Selfish.

I could lie my way out of this. I could tell her that 'Father' is a rank given to a certain level of Senior Mentor in the Research City and that this book was presented to me after I'd finished an important thesis on radiation poisoning. I could keep her world intact for moments longer. But she's staring at me with those eyes that see and I promised myself I wouldn't lie to her.

I swallow. She still hasn't taken her eyes off me.

'Please tell me.'

My resolve hardens. I won't be destroying Eden. This place is about as far from Eden as anywhere could be. And her world isn't intact. I'm here because of the interview she made – she has already seen the cracks, deduced the lies.

'People aren't magically made by a Creator,' I begin quietly and quickly, leaning forward, not that I believe we are being overheard, but more out of recognition of the rules that I am breaking. 'They come from other people. A male – a father, and a female – a mother.'

'No,' she's shaking her head firmly. Too fast. 'Animals are born from other animals. Not us. That's what sets us apart. We are made by the Creator. He gives us our bodies. He assigns us our numbers. In the past they broke his rules so he punished us by sending the radiation and allowing the Wilderness. We follow his rules now.' She trots it out. Knowledge, rote learnt, drilled in as a child.

'No,' I reply slowly and calmly, putting my hands on her shoulders to still the shaking. 'It's not true. You were made in a vessel but you came from…' I search for the words, words she'll understand… 'seeds from a male and a female. People. Other humans.'

She's shaking less now but her skin is even paler than normal and I fight back the urge to stroke the thin blue veins standing out in her hands.

'Have you met your father, then?' she asks. 'Your mother?'

'Yes,' I reply.

She looks at the floor and starts scratching at her left hand with her right. Scratching over and over, leaving red lines all over it as she begins to draw blood.

Finally, she looks up again, thoughts visibly whirring across her forehead.

'Why haven't I met mine?'

ALBA

I can't breathe properly. My ribcage is still moving in and out but it's like someone has tied an elastic band round my lungs, stopping them from filling up properly.

I don't want to believe him, but he has no reason to lie. He's sitting there, sweating and his eyes are dancing around in his head. He didn't mean to tell me. That clearly wasn't his plan. Guilt and fear are written all over his face. No, it's something he let slip out. Something I'm not supposed to know.

We're not created. The Creator doesn't magically form us, number us and then set us upon the earth. We come from people. Somewhere out there, there is a man and a woman whose cells made me. People I've never met.

Everything we've been told. Everything we do is to serve the Creator. The laws of Creation. We recite them first thing in the morning. They adorn the walls of the dorms. All the Guardians and the Supervisor do is lie to us. This place is full of lies. Pull one strand and the whole place unravels. The geese. The food. The whole Wilderness. This. It's toxic. My skin's crawling and itching and I want to run and scream and cry. I don't know in what order.

It doesn't make sense. Why does he know about Mothers and Fathers? Why has he met his while here we're being lied to?

Why? Why? Why? The word screams and echoes in my head.

'Why haven't I met mine?' I ask. My voice is small and wavering and I despise it for its weakness.

Arthur opens his mouth to answer but there's a rap on the door and the handle's turning.

'Just a minute,' calls out Arthur sharply.

The door handle freezes.

He leans in to me again.

I start to ask another question but he interrupts.

'Do you trust me?' he asks.

'Yes,' I reply without hesitation. He's the only person who's ever told me the truth about anything. At this moment he's the only person in the whole world I trust.

'Good,' he says. 'I will never lie to you. And I'm going to get you out of here,' he adds, almost angrily, a tiny muscle in his cheek pulsing. 'Away from all of this.'

'Do you promise?' I ask. I don't know why, but I need him to say it. To hear him say the words.

'I promise.'

His lips are centimetres from mine. I feel the warmth of his breath on my face. And suddenly he's leaning further in towards me and I'm leaning further in towards him. I don't mean to, it's just happening. Like gravity. And then his nose brushes past my nose and his lips are touching my lips and they're both rough and soft and kind and urgent and hungry, and inside I start melting again. Melting and melting until the rest of the room disappears and all there is in the universe is warmth and darkness and the feeling of his lips on mine.

'Very cosy in here.'

The words shatter the moment and bring the room back into sharp relief.

We spring guiltily apart as the Supervisor stands in the doorway, hands on hips. The temperature of the room drops.

Arthur stands.

'Yes, well, I'll be back tomorrow. Same time.'

'For your final visit before…?' the Supervisor says with a sneer, leaving the 'before' lingering in the air.

My heart leaps. Tomorrow's Thursday. That means he must be taking me away on Friday. I only have to survive forty-eight more hours here.

Arthur leaves the room, a formal nod in my direction as he pauses at the door, and then, when it's closed, the Supervisor roughly pulls me up to standing.

'This is my chair. Nobody else sits in my chair.'

I begin to apologise but then swallow the words. This woman will soon have no power over me. She's a liar and doesn't deserve my apology.

'Careful how you touch me,' I say. 'You're not my mother.'

ARTHUR

I've booked the window table at Jacques'. The one in the corner with the best view over the river. It's Father's favourite. You can see St Paul's on a fine day. Not today, though. Today low-lying cloud clings to the city, shrouding the buildings and turning the Thames grey.

Open and breathing on a side table is a bottle of St-Émilion, also Father's favourite, and I called ahead to reserve their two best rib-eye steaks. I am as prepared as I can be. I've even combed my hair and put on a suit. Father's always believed that *a smart appearance reflects a smart mind*. Briefly, I close my eyes, just for a minute, and remember the feel of Alba's lips on mine. The taste of her mouth. And it gives me strength.

Father arrives late. He has a word with the maître d' at the entrance, smiles benevolently at him and then walks towards our table. Nothing out of the ordinary or particularly flamboyant, but there's something about the way that he holds himself, the way he claims the space, that makes everyone turn to stare at him and whisper. He never just walks into a room. He always makes an entrance.

Once at the table, Father pulls back the chair and sits down, smooths the unwrinkled table cloth in front of him and then looks me directly in the eye. It feels like the table width shrinks in half.

'So, son, what's all this about? Linda said you were being evasive on the phone.'

I'd hoped to make small talk first. Ease my way in.

'How about a drink?' I say, gesturing to the side table. 'I've ordered the St-Émilion you like. And Jacques has reserved his two best steaks.'

Father doesn't smile, or make appreciative noises. I sound desperate to please which makes me weak. Father despises weakness. I've played this all wrong.

'Just a mineral water for me, thanks. It's only one after all,' he says, calling over the waiter and snubbing me in a single gesture.

I'm left with a whole bottle of very expensive wine to myself, feeling like a fool. Still, I can't afford to dwell. This is the most important conversation I'm ever going to have with Father. And it hasn't even begun.

'As you know, I've visited Centre 6,' I begin.

'More than once, I gather,' Father cuts in. 'Just the one Host though. If I remember rightly, you said you were deciding between two potential candidates. I fail to see why a choice of one should take so long.' I clench my fists under the table. I should have known someone from the

Centre would report back. The Supervisor most likely. Father has his spies everywhere.

Father adjusts his shirt collar. This is the precursor to his stretching his neck. An indicator that he's starting to store tension and that the clock is ticking.

'This Host is quite eye-opening,' I say, trying to keep my tone neutral, a rational observer, no more. 'She's extremely intelligent, adept at assimilating new information—'

'They all are,' Father interrupts impatiently. 'They're bred to be the perfect processor.'

'No!' I say and the words come out too loudly. The couple on the nearest table to our right stop eating and look over in alarm. I apologise and rein in my temper. Father hates any fuss that he hasn't instigated.

'She's more than that. She's clever and kind and thoughtful and—'

Father starts to shake. Silently at first. And then less so. A laugh escapes his lips and then builds in volume. Louder and deeper until it's all-consuming. Laughing so hard that the table is rocking and his knife is vibrating against its adjacent fork with a sharp, harsh clinking sound.

'What's so funny?' I ask, not bothering to disguise my irritation.

'My son, heir to the largest corporation in the Northern

Hemisphere, has fallen in love with a Host. A computer on legs. Fine, shapely, head-turning legs no doubt, but my point still stands.'

He stops laughing as abruptly as he started.

'You're making a fool out of yourself. Which means you're making a fool out of the company. Which reflects ill on me. End this nonsense, Arthur. Transition. Go ahead, have your minor act of rebellion and download into a female body. Shock me. Irritate me. At this point I no longer care. But this absurdity. These visits. This emotion. This ends now.'

I rack my brains for logical arguments to dissuade him but stumble upon none. There's nothing left. I have to appeal to him as a business man. Submit to the complete power over me that he's always craved.

'If you let her go, let her leave the Centre, I will do anything you ask for,' I say. 'I will spend all my time at M.A.D.E.' His face is expressionless. I have to try harder. 'I will attend every function as your son.' Still nothing. I'm desperate now and my mind is jumping around. There must be something I can offer. Something that will convince him to save her, even it if at the cost of everything I've worked for all these years. My one remaining moral thread. 'I will abandon the vaccine research programme. For real, this time. I will concentrate entirely on any field of your choosing.'

'You overestimate your usefulness,' he says snidely.

Debasing myself isn't working. I scramble around for one final tactic. What's the one thing, the only thing that has ever bothered him? Mother. That's it.

I lean forward, narrowing the space between us even more and stare him directly in the eye. I want there to be no mistake as to the seriousness of what I'm going to say next.

'If you don't let her go, I will kill myself. Just like Mother. That won't look good will it? A man whose wife and son both can't stand him. Can't stand to be alive around him.'

A muscle is pulsing in Father's jaw. I feel a tiny spark of triumph. I've got to him at last.

Then he leans in and we're almost as close as I was to Alba just before I kissed her.

'You won't be able to kill yourself. I know you're weak, unstable. Just like your mother. That's why I keep track of you. That injection. Your 'immunity booster'. The one that hurt a surprising amount...'

I'm back on edge. How does he know? I never told him that the injection hurt. I didn't report the nurse. I never even told Tommy.

'The needle was larger than normal to accommodate the tracker I had placed inside you. It monitors your vitals. Pulse rate, oxygen levels, blood toxicity.'

He pulls a small black display monitor out of his pocket. It's similar to the watch that's strapped around his wrist. A number in green in the top left-hand corner of the monitor flashes. 120. 121. 122.

'Your heart rate is accelerating, Arthur. As is your breathing. Do you feel anxious?'

The room is reeling.

'Dr Peters warned me you had reacted badly so I knew I had to keep an eye on you,' he continues. 'Try anything, and I'll get someone there to stop it.'

'You wouldn't get there in time,' I say but I can feel the fight draining out of me.

'Oh, but I would. You see, you're never alone. There's always someone out there following you. Watching. Waiting in the wings.'

Images come back in flashes. I think of the people in the street. The silver sedan. The footsteps in the alley. The arm pulling me out of the bar. I wasn't being paranoid. Father's speaking the truth. I was being followed all this time.

'And when they reach you, I'll decide who you come back as. Because come back you will. Again and again and again.'

Father clicks his neck and then continues, his voice softer now. The tone a simulacrum of paternal concern.

'What did you think was going to happen, Arthur?

That I'd let your Host girlfriend go and you would bring her back here to live with you happily ever after. Marry her? What do you think you'd tell her? That she'd been farmed so that people like you could download into her? That her friends had been wiped and that other people now inhabited their bodies? That you were about to die of a brain tumour so would have to pick a victim yourself and then come back looking completely different to the man she'd met? Did you really think that she'd accept this? Did you really think that she would forgive you? Did you really think that she could *love* someone like that?'

The room is swimming now. Shapes and people blurring and dissolving. I grip the edges of the table.

What hurts the most isn't even his refusal. His inability to grant the only thing I'd ever asked of him. It's that he is right.

Father is right.

Alba could never love a person like me.

ALBA

I'm starving. Lunchtime came and went without a Guardian turning up with a tray of food. I watched the clock: twelve, one, two – nothing. I don't think they forgot. I think it's intentional. The Supervisor's doing. A punishment for my earlier outburst. It was worth it though. The look on her face when I said the word 'mother'. Her realisation that I was seeing through all her lies. That Arthur trusted me enough to tell me the truth. That he's going to get me out of here.

I distract myself by reading. It's hard at first. The pages are faded and the dust still makes me sneeze, but then the story catches me and transports me away. I imagine I'm on a whaling ship, sailing far, far away from here. To the edge of the horizon, Arthur at my side.

Arthur.

I close my eyes and remember. His breath warm and soft as he leaned in towards me. The way the air seemed to be alive and spark with static. The excruciating slowness of his lips moving towards mine and then the feeling of contact. The heat. The feeling of falling. The solidity of his shoulders as they enveloped mine. Like his whole body was a shield that could wrap round and protect me.

Arthur. Strong as a bear.

ARTHUR

I stand in the middle of Waterloo Bridge and stare down at the swirling grey waters below, their depths dark and impenetrable. It's strange to think that there might be fish there, salmon even, swimming in the slate. I hold onto the railing, my grip so hard it's turning my knuckles white. My brain plays with the idea of throwing myself off. A dramatic dive. Arms outstretched like an Olympic competitor. Smashing into the water. Coldness. Then oblivion. But I know it's just a game. Even if I wanted to, someone, somewhere is waiting to dive in after me. There's a man in a navy raincoat who's spending too long tying his shoe. Is it him? Or the woman on the other side with a dog, pausing even though the dog does not appear to be relieving itself. Maybe her? In any event, what good would it do? Even if I manage to slip their notice, it doesn't help Alba. She'd still be taken. She'd still be erased. Someone else placed inside. Her eyes may reopen but they won't be hers. They won't see.

Shaking slightly I step back from the edge.

The clouds perforate and a fine drizzle hangs in the air. Tiny droplets form and then chase each other down my overcoat. I watch as they drip onto my shoes. A taxi stops on the road next to me, but I wave it on. I need to clear my head and a walk will do me good. My phone is flashing with messages from Tommy. Five missed calls. I turn it off. There's no point speaking to him. He doesn't understand.

Amidst all the confusion there is one certainty. Tomorrow I'll return to the Centre. Tomorrow I'll see Alba again. The thought gives me a surge of positivity. A purpose in this grey, damp squid of a world.

Alba.

I will work out how to save her.

There must be a way.

There must be.

ALBA

Trying to ignore my growling stomach, I sit and watch the sun set through the window. It doesn't get properly dark though. There's a full moon and it's enough to see for miles. Out beyond the walls of the compound, down the road and into the Wilderness beyond. Or to whatever's really there. To wherever Arthur's from. Curly suddenly pops into my head and I feel a rush of guilt that I haven't thought about her all day. Nor yesterday, for that matter. All my attention has been on Arthur. I'll see her soon, I tell myself. Arthur's taking me away. I'll go and find her. It'll be the first thing I do.

Curly will know about the Wilderness too. She's driven through it. She'll have learnt why they're lying to us and keeping us here. There'll be a reason. There's always a reason.

And she'll like Arthur, I know it. I imagine introducing them, showing him off. Her being a bit in awe of him to start with as everyone seems to be and then me saying, *Relax Curly, he's actually really sweet.*

And he'll like her. Everyone likes Curly. A tiny bit of me is worrying that maybe he'll like her too much, when there's a furtive knock at the door and the handle twists open.

Guardian Rich is standing uneasily in the door frame. His shoulders are slightly hunched over and his skin is an unhealthy greyish colour. He looks like he's aged years in the space of a few days. With a darting glance to each side, he enters, carrying a tea towel-wrapped bundle.

'Here, you must be hungry,' he whispers, thrusting the parcel into my hands. He's not meant to be here. In my room. Everything about the way he's behaving makes that completely clear. I open the tea towel to find a loaf of bread, a huge chunk of cheese, five thick slices of ham and two apples. It's enough food for a couple of days rather than two meals.

'Thanks,' I say and my stomach gurgles its approval. I try to smile as I know he's risked loads of trouble smuggling this in for me, but the corners of my mouth barely lift. The old openness we used to have is gone. He lied to me as much as the others did. And the lies hurt more as he'd pretended to be my friend.

I go to break off a piece of bread but he takes it from me and starts to rewrap the bundle. I don't understand. Was the food just a trick? Some sort of joke? If so, I don't get it.

'Alba,' he whispers urgently. 'You need to leave here, get away from this place.' His whole face is creased with concern and a little bit of my anger towards him thaws.

'I am leaving,' I say. 'Arth— the Mentor is taking me away on Friday.'

Guardian Rich does a little, brittle sort of cough laugh and shakes his head.

He doesn't believe me. And the anger's back.

'I didn't help Curly,' he says. 'But I can help you.'

'Like you helped me when I told you about the geese?' I snap back.

'I didn't tell anyone, Alba, it was your video.'

He's deliberately missing the point.

'Like you helped me when you lied to me year after year about the Wilderness? About us being made by a Creator? *The Creator sees everything. The Creator hears everything. Praise be to him.'* The words fly out like shrapnel and he winces as if he'd been hit.

'I'm sorry,' he murmurs. 'It's this place. It's a bad place.'

And it's my turn to laugh, a dark throaty, mocking laugh I hardly even recognise.

He cowers again before taking a deep breath and then starts to speak. His words come thick and fast, the spaces between them designed to be too small to allow for interruptions.

'There's a window at the far end of this corridor that can be forced open. It's a three-metre drop down from there, but you should be able to make it if you hang from your hands before you jump. There's a downpipe. It'll take your weight so you should make use of that as well. Once outside, head for the vegetable patches. The compound wall is weakest there. The surface has been weathered and the bolts stand out more than they should so you can use them to gain purchase to scale it. Be careful crossing the top because of the spikes. Once on the other side stay away from the main road but keep it in your sight. Use it to navigate. The moon will be enough to let you see, but it'll also make you easier to spot, so stay in the shadow of the trees. The road will eventually take you to a town. Ask for help. Someone will help you. Trust the people with face masks on. Only them.'

He's starting to scare me now. His urgency. The way he's talking. The detail. It isn't some sort of joke or random idea. He's planned it. He is serious. His eyes wild with intensity.

'And what about you?' I ask. I still don't trust him. 'What would they do to you if they find out you've let me out? They would find out. You know they would.'

'You can knock me out with that.' He points to the lamp on the desk. 'It'll look like you overpowered me. Hit me hard on the side of the head. But not so hard that it fractures the skull.'

He is still serious. The intensity undimmed.

I swallow and in that instant I know he means it – that he'd do this for me.

'I don't need to run,' I say, but more hesitantly this time. 'Arthur's going to take me out the front door.'

'There isn't a front door,' Guardian Rich replies. 'There's only a basement.'

'OK, *basement* door then.' Now's not the time for splitting hairs.

His eyes are moist as he takes hold of my arm. His fingers are rough and he holds on too tight. There's something in the way he's looking at me that I haven't seen before. Something that I hadn't even realised existed before I met Arthur. Guardian Rich wants to touch me. He wants to press his lips against mine.

'Let go!' I say and he flinches away.

'He's not what you think he is,' he hisses. 'He's sick, Alba.'

'He cares about me,' I fire back, wanting to get away from him. Far, far away.

'No, he wants to become you. He's booked it in. Set the date. This Friday, did you know that?'

'You're lying,' I reply, still backing away. I don't understand his words.

'Alba…'

'You're just jealous.'

He recoils slightly. I've hit a nerve.

He stares at his knees for the count of three and then looks up again. The fire has gone out of his eyes and he just looks tired.

'If he's so great then ask him to show you the basement, Alba. First thing tomorrow, ask him to show you that.'

He leans forward one more time and I flinch again.

And with that he holds his head in his hand before standing up and shuffling out of the room.

'I tried,' he murmurs almost to himself as he closes the door. 'At least I tried.'

I'm left staring out of the window again. Staring at the trees, their claw-like shadows long and monstrous in the moonlight.

I trust Arthur.

I think Guardian Rich is lying.

But then a little voice in my head starts nagging, 'Why would Guardian Rich risk everything to get you to run away?' Was it so that he could follow me and have me to himself? So that he wouldn't lose me to Arthur? But then wouldn't he run away with me rather than asking me to knock him out?

And how well do I really know Arthur? If there isn't a Wildernesss, there probably isn't a Research City. So why am I here? Why on earth am I here?'

I don't know who to believe. I don't have anyone to talk to. Curly, where the hell are you? I need you. I need you so much!

My mind tick tocks between trust and fear.

I don't sleep.

ARTHUR

The silver sedan no longer bothers to keep its distance. Father must have told his minions that I was onto them. It sits on my tail all the way to the Centre and then parks on the grass just before the drive dips underground. I can't see the guy's face. All I know is that he's a DMW. He's wearing a mask and his gloved hands grip the wheel. What's Father offered him, I wonder? The chance to become a Level One if he saves my life? That would be his normal style. Ensuring complete loyalty by dangling the unattainable on a stick. He probably wouldn't even make good on his promise if the situation arose. He has forceful ideas about the 'sort of person' who should be admitted to the club.

I walk through the car park to the basement door, eyes drinking in every detail. I need a plan and, as Father always says, 'The devil's in the detail.' He should know. I'm early, as planned, so they're not expecting me. I hold my finger to the entry pad and the light switches from red to green and the basement door opens. Good, I still have full access.

I stalk through the basement corridor and summon the lift at the end. So far so good.

The lift rises and its doors empty me out into the main corridor, ground level. The Supervisor's Assistant looks slightly harassed and out of breath as she's standing there, ready to greet me. So there's CCTV in the lifts. I wonder if it feeds to security, if they even have security, or just straight to her office.

She ushers me forward, towards the Supervisor's Office and we stride into the lair of the beast. The Supervisor's there, behind her desk, and she looks at me with a glint of amusement in her eye as she rises, fractionally later than is polite. She has lost her fear of me. She must have discovered I have less power than she thought.

'Forgive me,' she says, anything but apologetically. 'I forgot the time.' Then she looks pointedly at the clock, the hands at ten to eleven.

'I realise I'm early,' I say calmly. 'I can wait outside. I do not wish to inconvenience you.'

'No inconvenience at all,' she smiles and her teeth call to mind a tray of ice cubes. 'Please remind me, when is transition scheduled?'

As if she doesn't know. I want to strike her but instead I bite my tongue and do not let her know that she is getting to me.

'Tomorrow.'

'So this is your last visit?'

'Yes.'

My refusal to rise to the bait deprives her of the entertainment she seeks so she asks her assistant to 'Fetch F3527' and then stalks out the room.

I sit and watch the door.

Waiting for Alba to arrive.

Willing her here.

Minutes stretch and drag and then, finally, there's a knock at the door.

It opens and she's standing there.

I smile, it's a reflex reaction. I see her and my heart lifts, taking the corners of my mouth with it. I want to hold her, pull her close and kiss her again and again and forget that the rest of the world exists.

It takes me a moment to register that she's not smiling back. She's just standing there, her face pale, her cheeks hollow, staring at me with those eyes that see.

ALBA

He's sitting in the same leather armchair as before. His eyes look up at me like he's drinking me in. I want to walk over to him. To touch him. Stroke his cheek. Kiss him. But I can't. I can't weaken. I have to know. To finally understand.

I take a deep breath.

'Show me the basement,' I say.

I hope he's going to look confused. To wrinkle up his forehead or laugh or say something like: *What do you mean? Why the basement? Are you feeling OK? What's up, Alba?*

But he doesn't. He says nothing, but all the colour drains from his skin and his eyes suddenly have this haunted quality.

In that second I know that Guardian Rich wasn't lying. That something terrible is happening here. I'd thought the issue was the lies. The radiation that wasn't. The Wilderness that isn't. But that isn't the issue, not at all. Something far worse is going on. Something that all the lies had been invented to cover up.

'I want to see the basement,' I say again, my voice louder this time. More forceful.

I stare at him and refuse to look away. He blinks and looks down at his shoes.

'You told me you wouldn't lie to me. You promised,' I choke out. I've started crying and I don't know why. 'You have access, don't you?'

He pauses and then nods slowly, eyes red-rimmed, mirroring my own.

'Then show me. If you care anything about me at all. If this, us, hasn't all been a lie. *Show me.*'

He slowly stands and wraps his hand round mine and then we're walking out of the office. The Supervisor's Assistant looks up, startled as we pass.

'Um… Mr Easton, sir, does the Supervisor know that you're … um leaving?'

He silences her with a glare. 'Need I remind you that I'm the heir to the M.A.D.E. corporation. We own this Centre. We own all the Centres. Does it look like I need anyone's permission?'

She squirms in her seat as if trying to burrow her way into it and away from his wrath.

'No, sir. Of course not, sir.'

We walk down the corridor. It's empty – everyone's outside or in classes, and the sound of our footsteps bounces off the walls. We stop in front of the lift. There's no one else there to witness as he places his finger against the call pad. No one else to see as we walk inside.

The doors close, swallowing us and we begin to descend. My stomach drops.

'Alba...' Arthur pulls me round to face him. 'You need to understand that I was never going to hurt you. That I ... love you.'

We both freeze.

'Sorry,' he continues quietly. 'I hadn't intended to tell you like this. I'd wanted to wait till we were out of here. Somewhere romantic. Private. Never in a place like this. But it's the truth nonetheless. I'd told myself I was falling for you. That it was a crush. But it's more than that. I've fallen. I'm on the floor. I love you.'

I looked at him properly this time and saw that his eyes were dulled by sorrow.

'And what you're going to see isn't...' His voice cracks. 'It isn't ... me.'

I don't reply. It's all too much. I've disengaged. I'm here but not here. A tangle of nerve fibres. Eyes and ears attached to a brain. Looking. Hearing. Evaluating.

The lift stops moving and the doors on the other side open.

I take a tentative step forward and automatic lights turn on revealing a smart marble corridor in front, a door set in it halfway down the right-hand side. There are photos and flowers. It is luxurious beyond anything I've ever seen. Like the inside of a hotel from a design book in the library.

Arthur's grip on my hand tightens. I hadn't even realised he was still holding it.

At the far end of the corridor I can make out a grey metallic door. That must be it. The gateway to freedom. To outside.

I swallow, confused. I don't get it. I don't know quite what I'd been expecting but this wasn't it. Everything is strangely clinical but ... evil? I steal a glance at Arthur. He's standing, rigid, next to me, the vein in his neck pulsing. He knows something. What does he know?

His eyes are resolutely fixed on the metallic door at the far end.

'Come with me now,' he says suddenly, excitedly tugging at my hand. 'I have clearance. I can open that door and we can leave this place. We can drive away. Far away. A man may try and stop us. If he does, I'll try and distract him and you run. Run and don't stop.'

I want to say yes. Every bit of my body wants to say let's do it. Let's run away now. But now that I'm here, in the basement, I realise I have to know the truth first. I need to know why I'm here. Why the rest of us are here. What the point of it all is.

As if he can read my mind, Arthur says, 'I'll explain everything. Leave with me now, before we're missed, before anyone can stop us and I'll explain it all. No one will ever lie to you again.'

But the trouble with having been lied to for so long is that you end up not fully trusting anyone. You need to see things for yourself. With your own eyes.

I stare around the basement for a moment. Trying to put my finger on what's making me feel so on edge. Then it hits me. I'd been expecting a huge storage area not this glamorous corridor. After all, everyone knows that the hazmat suits are stored in the basement. That's why we weren't allowed down here. In case you did something and the suits got ripped or damaged so they no longer locked out radiation.

'Where are the hazmat suits?' I ask, but mid-asking I realise that there's an opening to a second unlit corridor off to my left and think – oh, he's going to say down there so, I'm only half listening when he replies, 'There are no hazmat suits.' He sounds resigned now, defeated. He's let go of my hand.

I curse myself for being an idiot. Of course there are no hazmat suits. There's no Wilderness. No hazmat suits required. I've got to get my brain in gear but it's really hard to shake a lifetime of being lied to.

I stare at the unlit corridor again.

'So what's down there?' I ask, my voice now shrunk to little more than a whisper.

Arthur looks at me with the saddest of eyes and then says, 'I don't know. Honestly, I don't.'

He takes my hand again as if to say we'll look together.

We edge into the second corridor, padding at the wall with our hands to find the light switch. I find it, and flickering strip lights on the ceiling hum into life. This corridor is lined with concrete rather than marble and there is a door off on either side, a metal trolley discarded at an angle at the end.

We stop outside the door on the left. It's locked and Arthur presses his finger against the access panel. It turns from red to green and then opens with a click.

The room has no windows. It's little more than a large storage cupboard. The lights take a moment to reach full intensity and reveal the room's contents. Against one wall rests a broom and a mop. There's something else at the back. A shape. A heap of something. The light continues to build and my eyes begin to focus. Even then it takes me a moment to understand. It's a pile of bags. A pile of dark grey, square, canvas bags. Bundled, one on top of the other. Several hundred or more. Some plain, some with small, embroidered patches of colour.

No. It can't be. No.

I suddenly feel numb as my heart rate spikes. *BOOM. BOOM. BOOM.*

'Alba—'

I turn to look at him. His face is pale and taut, a mask of confusion. He tries to put his arm around me but I throw it off and now I'm running, running towards the heap. Checking bag after bag. Looking until I find it. I don't need to search for long. It's near the top. The embroidery makes it easy to find. A red rose. A green leaf that curls round and round like a secret signature. Curly's.

I rip the bag open. Even now I'm telling myself, maybe they decided it was easier if people left their bags behind and just carried their things with them. Maybe that's what Curly did. But now the bag's open and nestled inside is the clay vase and photo and comb. She would never have willingly left without them. Never. They were her things. Her memories. Us.

My breath is coming short and fast as I back away from the pile, my vision blurring.

What does it mean? What does it mean?

I spin round and Arthur's there. His eyes are red and a muscle is jumping in his neck. He looks as horrified as I feel.

'I'm so sorry,' he says. 'I didn't know. I swear it.'

This anger comes over me and I start to pummel at his chest with my fists. Over and over. I'm crying and hitting and crying and finally, when my arms are shaking too much to carry on, I look up and notice that he's crying too.

'Why?' I ask, between sobs. 'Why make them pack a bag just to throw it away again? Why do that?'

'I imagine it's to keep everyone calm,' he says. 'So that no one suspects or questions.'

All I can think of is the look that must have been on Curly's face as she reached the basement and they took her precious bag from her. When she first knew it was all a lie.

'Show me the next room,' I demand, roughly brushing away tears. 'I need to see. I need to know everything.'

Arthur leads and I follow. The second door on the right is different. It's thicker. And the opening is wider. The metal trolley, or bed on wheels – whatever it is – leans against the wall just beyond it.

He places his finger to the entrance pad and I hear the same click as before. This time, however, I have to strain to get the door to move at all. Finally, it starts to open with a strange 'whoosh'. I stare at the door frame and door and realise they're both lined with soft plastic or rubber or something to create a sort of seal. The whoosh must have been the sound of air escaping as the seal broke.

'Why...?' I start to ask but, as soon as I'm inside the room, I answer my own question.

Because of the smell.

The air makes me gag and I have to lift my tunic over my mouth and nose to block the scent. It's sickly sweet, oily and charred. The same smell there was when they roasted Roly. The same smell that there is every time the wind changes direction and blows over the Wilderness.

My mind glitches.

But there is no Wilderness.

Then I take in the rest of the room and everything falls into place. And I start laughing. Laughing and I can't stop. I'm hysterical.

Arthur looks at me, scared.

He doesn't get I'm laughing at myself. At what a fool I've been. A stupid little gullible fool.

Against the back wall there's a stainless-steel cuboid with a huge silver door and a pipe snaking up the wall then out to wherever.

It's an oven. A large oven.

The smell from the Wilderness always came after someone had been chosen.

That's why Guardian Rich had wanted me to leave. That's why he'd looked so upset after Curly'd been chosen.

They kill us.

They killed Curly.

They were going to kill me.

I turn to Arthur and stare him dead in the eye.

'You're monsters.'

ARTHUR

It was better when she was hitting me. I wanted her to. God knows I deserved it. And the better part of me was hoping that her fists would in some way transfer her pain to me. I'd take it all. Anything for her.

The raw horror of this place.

It is like I've been blind my whole life but now my eyes are open. Eyelids pulled back and gripped by a vice, unable to ever reclose.

I'd seen everything through a protective filter before. Through the intentionally calming removal afforded by the company sales materials and their corresponding lexicon – 'Selection', 'Host', 'Centre', 'Transition'. Words chosen for their innocuous sound. For their lack of humanity and absence of messy emotion.

I've been to basements before, obviously, three of them in fact, but only to their Transition Room and even then it was always after the Host – person, victim – had already been sedated and screened off. I'd never seen the second corridor. The other rooms. The apparatus. The lies and cruelty and cold efficiency that holds it all together. Hope deflated and then discarded in a pile of grey bags.

She's right.

We're monsters.

Absolute monsters.

'Why?' she asks, fixing me with those piercing eyes. 'I don't get it. Why bother? Why waste all this time and energy raising us, educating us, making us take these tests and medicals and do all these interviews if you're just going to kill us. *Burn* us. Is it all a game to you?'

I try to speak but she interrupts immediately.

'And me ... getting to know me. Telling me you *love* me. Is that just an extra level of the game that the high-up people get to play?'

Her words slice me.

'It's not a game,' I reply, begging her to recognise the sincerity in my voice. 'You were never a game. I do love you.'

'But,' her arms are flailing round, '*Why?*' She's pleading now, desperate to understand.

'We don't burn you,' I say. I don't know how to make it sound any better. But she deserves the truth. It's the least I can give her. 'It's my body that would be burnt.'

She freezes. It's not what she was expecting me to say.

'Follow me,' I say. 'There's one more room. Then you'll understand.'

ALBA

We're back in the marble tiled section again, standing in front of the final door. This door is lighter again and glides open easily after Arthur touches the entry pad.

My mind is scrambling, trying to run through possible explanations, scenarios, to bring it all together, but none make sense and my efforts are just pulling me down into an internal black hole. I have to concentrate. The truth lies in this room.

Lights come on automatically. The room is bigger than the other two. The floor is polished wood and the walls are lined with bland but tasteful prints of ferns and trees and birds. This room clearly gets a different sort of visitor. A more important sort of visitor.

But for what?

The centre of the room is taken up by a large machine that looks a bit like the computers we have upstairs. There's a central monitor connected to a huge enclosed section covered in dials and sprouting leads. It's not on. None of the lights are glowing.

On either side of the machine are two metal armchairs, facing each other as if in conversation. One of them has arms with metal circles at the end. The other doesn't. The backs of the chairs are unlike any I've seen before. They're weirdly high and protruding. At first I think they have headrests like the one Guardian 17 has on her chair when she teaches us Science. It's on account of her bad neck. But on closer inspection these aren't headrests. They're high metal domes. Hollow inside. They look more like helmets. Metal helmets. Each one is attached to a different point on the central computer by a long snaking lead.

I approach the nearest chair and run my hand over it. It's cold to the touch.

There's a knot in my stomach and I feel like I'm shrinking. That I'm getting smaller and smaller and will soon disappear.

'What is this?' I ask, unable to keep the tremor from my voice. 'What happens here?'

ARTHUR

I don't know how to begin so I just start talking, hoping that the words will catch up.

'Have you learnt about bacteria?' I ask.

She nods.

'Outside,' I say, waving my hand in the direction of the world beyond the Centre, 'people are dying. Bacterial infections have become so virulent and resistant to antibiotics that they are impossible to control. Important people didn't want to die. So they found a way not to.'

'I still don't understand,' she says, but the clouds forming in her eyes suggest that she is starting to.

'You, what makes you you – your thoughts, memories, dreams – can be reduced to electronic data. Your brain is basically a computer, a data processor. My father found a way to transfer this data from one brain to another so that the first person never really dies.'

'And the new brain? The new person?' she asks slowly, tracing the rim of the helmet with her finger. 'What happens to the *data* that was there?'

My mouth is dry and my tongue feels like it no longer fits inside my teeth. I force myself to answer her.

'It's wiped. The Host – the person – is wiped.'

'How can they do that? To another person?'

'They don't want to die. And they can. They do it because they can.'

Without taking her eyes off me, Alba walks round to the front of the chair and sits down. She lowers the helmet so that it's resting on the crown of her head.

I can't keep them in any more, tears are flooding down my cheeks.

'Is that what happened to Curly?'

It's my turn to nod.

'Someone … someone out there … is walking around inside Curly's body?'

I nod again and her eyes turn to fog, like Mother's after Father brought her back.

'And you are going to walk round in mine.'

It's a statement rather than a question and her whole body starts shaking. She's not crying. Just shaking. Like electric current is coursing through her body.

'No, I'm not going to let it happen,' I insist fiercely, trying to touch her hand. She flinches away. Suddenly she stops shaking and turns to stare up at me. Something else is troubling her. Finally, she breaks her silence.

'Why did I have to copy your handwriting?'

'I didn't know you had to,' I reply, confused. I think for a moment, then I work it out. The bastards. Efficient bastards. I share my theory. 'Muscle memory. So it feels natural writing in the same style in the new body.' I think back to the brochures. *Every attention is given to consistency of experience.*

'Why don't you stop them?' she asks. 'If you're as important as everyone seems to think, why don't you just say no?'

I sink into the chair opposite her and begin to tell her about Father. About Mother. About being followed. I try not to sugar-coat it. I know I could have ended things earlier. I didn't choose my first transition but I didn't resist the second. Or the third. I accepted them as inevitable. The impulse to live, to survive is very strong, it's ingrained into every cell. That's what we all tell ourselves, anyway. Maybe the simpler truth is that I'm selfish. Selfish and weak.

I don't look up until I've finished. I'm scared to see her face.

When I pluck up the courage, I can't quite determine her expression. The wariness is still there but some of the hostility is gone.

'I'm sorry about your mother,' she says.

'Thank you,' I reply

We're dancing round each other, not quite sure where to tread.

There's a long pause.

'Are you dying?' she asks. 'Is that why you're here?'

'Yes,' I reply quietly.

'I'm sorry,' she says again.

This time a fleeting look of compassion passes across her face and this hurts me more than anything. That this girl. This amazing, clever, kind girl could feel sorry for me after everything she's been put through.

She leans her head against my shoulder and I wrap my arm around her and in that moment I find peace.

ALBA

I don't understand the world. I don't understand anything. Here's a man who I should hate. Who belongs to bad, bad people. But try as I might, I don't hate him. I can't. He's suffered too. It's written on his face. No, not the face. The face has been stolen. It's written on his soul. He's been lied to too. I think I love him. I think, despite everything, I love him. The realisation almost makes me laugh. Laugh at the absurdity of life.

I lean my head against his shoulder and listen to his heart beat through his shirt and feel the warmth of his skin and somehow, despite everything, feel strangely at peace.

It doesn't last long.

Suddenly there's a noise from out in the corridor. Footsteps, raised voices – three different ones at least. One deep and booming, one sharp, one high-pitched. All three resonating alarm.

'Mr Easton?' comes the call. 'Mr Easton?'

We should have left. I should have listened to Arthur. We would have been far away from here by now. In a car down a road somewhere. Speeding. Not looking back.

Clang.

Somewhere out there a door is flung open.

Arthur wraps his arms round me tightly and kisses the back of my neck. I can't stop trembling.

'Let's get this over with,' he whispers. 'It's not all over. Everything's going to be OK.'

He begins to rise to his feet as the door to this room is thrown open. The three Guardians hesitate in the doorway, held back by their residual awe of Arthur's position.

'Inside,' a fourth voice barks from behind the wall of Guardians. I know that voice. The Supervisor.

Arthur moves to stand in front of me, his body a shield, but Guardian 11 elbows past and grabs me by the upper arms. He twists, pinning my arms behind my back and I squeal in pain.

'Let her go,' Arthur orders, but they ignore him. They don't lay a finger on him, but still, the balance of power has shifted.

The Supervisor stalks forward. 'So, Mr Easton. This has been quite the surprise. Did my office provide insufficient entertainment?'

Arthur stares at her, saying nothing, the loathing he feels clear in his gaze.

She places her hand on the back of the chair with the metal circles and then spins it round lightly.

'Or were you just showing F3527 where she was to sit tomorrow? Helping her adjust? How thoughtful of you.' She was positively purring now, the sound curdling in my stomach. 'You are still coming tomorrow, aren't you? Or need I organise a last-minute substitute if you've lost your appetite? There's always plenty of demand for a fully certified, high-scoring Host.'

I'm here. She's talking about me like I'm nothing. Like I'm an object. I'm here.

'I'll be here,' Arthur replies curtly.

The Supervisor glances round and seems confused to see me still in the room.

'Take her upstairs, one of you. Now.'

I'm pushed forwards, a short jab in the small of my back.

'Be careful with her,' Arthur shouts.

As they march me past him, he whispers, 'I'm getting you out, Alba. I swear it.' His tone radiates sincerity and I believe him. I don't know why, but I believe him.

I'm pushed out of the room, twisting my neck so far that it hurts for one last look at Arthur.

I feel his eyes on me, boring through walls to my skin, as I'm marched to the lift.

ARTHUR

'I need a gun.'

Tommy has the decency to look surprised as he quickly closes the door behind me.

'I'm very well, thanks, and how are you?' he replies, trying to sound amused but I can tell he's thrown. 'So you've woken me up from a rather pleasant afternoon snooze to tell me that you've cracked up?'

'No,' I bite back. 'Be serious, Tommy, please. 'I need to save this girl. And to do that I need a gun.'

I tell Tommy all about Father refusing to help, about the basement, about tomorrow being my last chance to get her out alive.

'Aren't you forgetting one thing, Arthur?' he says, fixing himself a large Scotch. He offers me the bottle but I decline. 'The tumour. You're dying, old chap. It's all very noble and chivalrous and what have you to rescue this girl, and I understand she means a lot to you, that she's got under your skin, but the fact remains that if you don't transition in the next few days, you, Arthur Easton, will die, and I for one would be eternally glum.'

'I've made up my mind,' I reply quietly. 'It's the right

231

thing to do. It's been too long since I've known what the right thing to do is.'

Tommy takes a large sip and then another, draining the glass. He stares at me, trying to judge if I can be dissuaded.

'Right, one gun,' he says, concluding that I can't. 'Anything else you need for this suicide mission?'

I think.

'Your car. And you. If you wait outside the door with the engine on, it'll increase our chances of escape.'

'Getaway driver, I like it,' Tommy says with a raffish smile.

I stay for a while and we chat. It's small talk. Nonsense. The tennis match he had earlier. Humphrey's new haircut. A potential holiday to Munich in the Spring. Anything but Hosts and transitioning and tomorrow. The words themselves don't matter, it's the warmth that underlines them.

Finally, I stand to leave. It's getting late and I need to be sharp tomorrow. Sharper than I've ever been.

'I best be going too,' Tommy drawls. 'Got to see a man about a gun.'

Tommy walks me to the door but then hesitates in the hallway, suddenly stiffening, his much-prized and affected loucheness gone. There's something he wants to tell me but he's having difficulty enunciating.

I wait, hoping the silence will coax it out.

'You know I'm a little bit in love with you, Artie, old chap,' he murmurs, his voice cracking with emotion.

I stare at him; his eyes aren't sparkling, they're deep, dark pools and I can see he's drowning in them.

I expect Tommy's revelation to catch me off guard, but it doesn't. In some way I think I've always known. I wish I could tell him what he needed to hear, but I can't. I love Tommy, but not in the way that he wants me to.

'I know there's nothing to be done about it, but I thought you should know.' Tommy tries to crack a smile. 'It seemed like the right time.'

I wrap my arms round his shoulders and squeeze.

'You're the best friend I've ever had,' I reply. 'My only true friend. I'm going to miss you so much.'

The hallway suddenly feels very quiet.

'Tommy?' I add.

'Yes?'

'If I get her out…'

'I'll look after her.'

'Thank you, Tommy, thank you.'

And he cracks his sad lopsided grin one more time.

ALBA

It's only the afternoon but I lie on the bed and try to sleep so I don't have to think about everything I've seen today. About what's going to happen tomorrow. But then the dreams come and they shake me awake, covered in sweat. Arthur's there, talking to me and then his form shifts and it's still his voice but now it's Curly standing in front of me, the words coming out of her mouth. Her eyes are dead and lifeless but the mouth is opening and closing like a puppet. Then everything shifts again and I'm standing in front of the big mirror that's in the medical room and it's still Arthur's voice I'm hearing but in the mirror it's now me that I'm seeing. My mouth that's moving in time. My eyes that are dead.

I've got pins and needles in my feet and it feels like there's a fist wrapped round my heart, squeezing.

I trust Arthur. I think I trust Arthur. He loves me. He says he loves me. I think he loves me. He says he'll get me out of here. But how? How will he get me past the Guardians, the Supervisor? It's hopeless.

Maybe he'll get home and realise it's all impossible and then he won't even try? Maybe he'll stay away and then they'll put someone else inside my head?

I'm not going to cry. Now's not the time to cry.

Shaking, I go to the window and try to force it open. It's impossible. It's screwed shut. I try forcing it again, biceps straining, fingers scraped raw from effort. Again, but it doesn't move.

I'm trapped. Trapped.

Think, brain, I tell myself. Think.

Then I remember Guardian Rich's whispered advice about the window down the corridor. The one that can be opened.

I unplug the desk lamp and wrap the cord around the base. Gripping it tightly in my right hand I stand to the left of the door frame and wait. Hoping that someone will come.

At 6pm there's a shuffling movement from outside the door and the handle begins to turn. It'll be a Guardian with dinner.

The door begins to open. A few centimetres. Now twenty. Now thirty.

And I'm jumping, barrelling towards the person coming in. They fall back with a yell and the tray's falling the other side of them, clattering onto the floor but I'm not focusing on that, I'm out the door and I'm running. The window's only ten metres away. Shouts behind me are getting louder. There's more than one voice now. And there are feet behind me, pounding along the floorboards. A drum war beat. I'm there. At the window. Fingers under the lower frame, heaving it open. The air is cold against my face, slapping me awake. I've never felt more alive.

I can do this.

My head's outside. My head is outside.

Victory fills me.

Then there are hands on my legs. Pulling, wrenching. And I'm back in the corridor and then a fist swings towards me.

Then blackness.

I awake sometime later. How much later, I don't know. I'm back in the room, chained to the leg of the bed. And I sit there, for the whole night. Too scared to close my eyes.

ARTHUR

Tommy's at the wheel. We drive in silence but still it's good to have him next to me.

'Let me be your chauffeur,' he'd insisted. 'You can call me James. It'll be fun.'

His mask of affected ease is back on but he seems to wear it looser now. More comfortably.

It's a beautiful day and Tommy's got the top down. I close my eyes and feel the sun on my face, knowing that fifty or so metres behind us a silver sedan is watching my every move.

Nestled on my lap is a leather satchel bag at the bottom of which sits a gun. I don't know what type. I know nothing about guns. It's a little bigger than my hand and silver. Tommy talked me through me how to load it. How to remove the safety and then how to pull the trigger. In theory, that is. We couldn't risk actually firing the thing and bringing the police down on our heads in a dawn raid.

I clutch the bag tighter. It's like I can feel the gun's cold metallic smoothness through the leather and I'm too wary to put it on the floor.

The burnt section of the forest seems to have grown

since last night and we drive through blackened stumps of bushes and brambles before turning into the final approach to the Centre. The barrier opens and then the driveway dips underground and we pull into the car park. Tommy stops in a space right next to the basement door.

'Do you want me to come in with you?' he asks.

I shake my head. He's risking enough driving me. I can't put him in any more danger. If I manage to pull this off, there will be a lot of very angry important people and heads will roll.

Three deep breaths and I'm at the door.

ALBA

I don't know what time Guardian 12 comes into my room carrying a bag. It's long past dawn though – the sun is fully up. This is it, I tell myself. This is the day I either escape or am erased.

I'm still sitting at the end of the bed – the chain round my wrist doesn't allow for much movement.

'No breakfast today,' Guardian 12 trills. 'The "procedure" can make people sick so it isn't advised.' They've stopped lying to me now at least. Now that they know I know. She has a cruel glint in her eyes as she's telling me this. Like she's enjoying it. I don't give her the satisfaction of reacting.

She stops in front of me, beaked nose pointed at mine, and pulls up my chin, examining my face carefully.

'Goodness,' she exclaims. 'We'll have to do something about this. Can't have an Easton waking up looking like this now, can we?' She laughs as if she's made the world's funniest joke and then seems almost a bit surprised that I'm not joining in.

She puts her bag down on the desk and unzips it. First she pulls out some more of Guardian 23's miracle cream and dots it into my face, rubbing it in in small concentric circles. She holds up a mirror so I that can see the transformation. I don't look.

Then she dives into the bag again and pulls out a black cylinder thing about 3cm wide and a bit longer than my hand with three metallic discs at one end.

'You'll have to sit still for this,' she explains. 'Normally we do it in the basement but it'll be easier for me to do a neat job up here without the distractions.'

What was she talking about? My stomach knotted tighter.

She switches the black thing on and it starts to hum. She then pulls up the right-hand side of my hair and presses it against my scalp. There is a strange pulling sensation and it feels like my whole scalp is vibrating. Long pieces of hair start to fall onto the bed quilt beside me and tumble down to the floor. My hair. She is shaving my hair.

I flinch away in horror and then wince as the razor cuts me.

Guardian 12's bony hand flashes out and slaps my arm. I am too stunned to react.

'Stay still,' she barks. 'It's not like I'm taking it all off. Just the bits at the side. It improves conductivity. It won't show when the hair's down.'

Stop with the explanations, I want to yell. *I don't want to hear about making it easier to wipe my brain or zap in other people's thoughts. I'm not an observer. This isn't an interesting lecture. This is happening to me. You're trying to destroy me.*

She moves onto the other side of my head and yet more brown tendrils come snaking down. I fight back the tears that prick at the corner of my eyes.

Guardian 12 stands again, brushing the remaining sides of my hair over the bald patches.

'Perfect. You'd never know,' she crows. 'Right, time to get you downstairs, then.'

ARTHUR

The door is opened before I even have a chance to place my finger on the entry pad. The Supervisor's smile is wider than normal. Snow piled up on the top of a mountain before an avalanche.

'Mr Easton. This way, please.'

She's flanked by two Guardians: one female and strong-looking with hair tucked behind her ears, the other male with round glasses and short grey hair. I haven't seen them before. I follow them in silence, clutching the leather bag close to my side, paranoid that they might somehow be able to gauge its contents.

The Supervisor opens the door to the Transition Room and I see her. Alba. She's already inside, standing next to the metal chair with clamps. Another female Guardian, beak-nosed and thin, hovers at her side. They've pinned Alba's hair up revealing two bald patches, one on either side of her head, just above her ears.

How dare they.

They haven't clamped her into the chair yet. Haven't screened her off. Haven't sedated her. Different emotions fight each other. Relief that she's not sedated. It'd be much harder to get her out of here if they had. And then anger that they haven't. They want her to feel. To see. To suffer.

My heart leaps against my ribcage. She looks tiny. Folded in on herself. I stare at her, trying to tell her without words that everything is going to be all right.

I want to rush over to her but I can't. I force my feet to remain planted in the corridor as the Supervisor and her two Guardian sidekicks enter the room. I need to time this perfectly. Glancing behind me I confirm that there are no more Guardians out in the corridor. Everyone else is inside – the Supervisor, the three Guardians and Alba.

Four to deal with.

One to save.

The Guardian next to Alba starts to force her into the chair.

I can't let them clamp her wrists. That'd slow us down and I couldn't hold the gun and unlock the clasps at the same time.

I need to act.

Now.

ALBA

The door's thrown open and I see him. He's here. Arthur's here at last. A seed of hope starts to germinate. He'll take me out of here. Away from this room. This chair. This helmet. He's not going to let them erase me.

I watch as he hovers in the doorway. But he's not coming into the room. Something's wrong. He's not meeting my eye. He's just standing in the corridor, looking around guiltily.

My mind starts to race. What's his plan? He doesn't look like someone with a plan. I'd imagined him storming in. Knocking everyone out of the way. Blowing open the doors and releasing hell. But he continues to just stand there. Doing nothing.

I can feel doubt creeping in, my heart starting to sink as my reality shifts once more. I trusted him. I can't believe I trusted him. *Fool.* He's one of them. The enemy. He's taken bodies before. He'll do it again. Take mine.

Emotion is spiralling up inside me and my legs start shaking. I can't control them. I can't make them stop.

'Sit down, Alba,' Guardian Rich instructs softly and I glare up at him. The traitor. After all his pretence of caring for me, of wanting me to escape, here he is at the end to make sure that I never will.

I force my arms up against the arms of the metal chair and keep my legs rigid. I'm not going to sit down. They are going to have to make me.

Guardian 12 starts pushing my legs, trying to force them to bend at the knee and I'm fighting back with all my strength, arching my back.

'It's pointless resisting,' the Supervisor snaps from the corner. 'You're only prolonging the inevitable.'

Guardian 12 pushes down again and I bite her upper arm as it passes my face. I taste blood and she slaps me.

I swivel my head again round the side of the chair to stare at Arthur. *Do something. Don't let me down. Please do something.*

And then he does.

'Everyone against the wall.' His voice is loud but measured. He's in control.

Guardian 12 lets go of my legs so I can turn round properly and I see Arthur standing there, inside the room now, with a gun outstretched. It's pointed straight at the Supervisor, aiming directly between her eyes.

The air in the room is suddenly alive. Static. Thoughts humming. Hearts racing.

Arthur releases the safety on the gun and there's a click.

The increased hum means that everyone's heard it.

'Against the wall,' he growls again.

They obey. Guardian Rich and Guardian 12 back away from the chair and stand against the far wall. The Supervisor and Guardian 17 join them, fury radiating off them.

A rogue's gallery in front of a bland display of fern prints.

Arthur has the upper hand but there might be cameras down here. Other Guardians watching upstairs ready to flood down and overpower us. There's no time to lose.

I run over to stand at Arthur's side. Edging backwards, gun extended, we leave the room. I kick the door to the Transition Room shut behind us and then we're sprinting to the large metal external door. The only thing standing between us and freedom.

They're not following. Not yet.

The light on the exit pad is red as Arthur raises his finger.

The door handle of the Transition Room starts to turn.

I push against the metal door. It makes a gong sound but doesn't move.

'The light's still red,' I hiss. 'Why is the light still red?'

'I don't know,' he whispers. 'It makes no sense.'

Turn green I beg the door. *Turn green now.*

ARTHUR

The door to the Transition Room opens and the Supervisor steps into the corridor.

'I see your father took my advice and downgraded your security clearance,' she smirks. 'A fugitive son is not a very good look for a corporation, is it?'

Witch, I scream inside my head. *Witch*. The walls are closing in on me and I can't breathe. I can't breathe. I need to save this girl. I promised I'd save this girl.

'Don't come any closer,' I say, aiming the gun at her. My hand is shaking. 'I will shoot. Stay where you are.'

The Supervisor hesitates for a moment, but then takes a step towards me. Her eyes glint as if she can sense weakness.

I fire a warning shot at the ceiling. At least I try to, but something goes wrong. There's no explosion, just a clicking sound. The trigger's stuck. I squeeze the trigger again. Still nothing. No explosion. No bullet.

I don't understand.

The bloody gun doesn't work.

Or maybe I'm doing something wrong. I've never even held one of these damned things before. I should have asked Tommy to talk me through it more slowly.

I try again.

Click.

The Supervisor's smirk becomes a grin.

'Guardians,' she screams. 'Out here now.'

ALBA

It's over.

It's all over.

The Guardians stream out of the Transition Room towards us. Guardians 12 and 17 grab Arthur's arms while Guardian Rich takes mine. I can't believe he's here and helping them. After everything he said about trying to get me out of here. Maybe my rejection of him was too much. This is his kind of sick revenge.

'My apologies for the manhandling, Mr Easton,' the Supervisor purrs. 'But your father was very clear that the transition was to happen today. By any means necessary. I believe those were his words.'

Arthur doesn't reply. He's not here. His body's here, obviously, but it's like his life force, his energy, his drive, has been sucked out of him.

I'm kicking and screaming and biting at the air as Guardian Rich forces me into the chair and then clamps me in. The metal clasps are tight against my skin and as much as I struggle, I can't move.

Arthur is sitting opposite, defeated. There are no clamps on his chair so Guardian 12 fashions some makeshift ones out of rope. He doesn't even struggle.

'I'm so sorry, Alba,' he whispers. 'I'm so sorry.'

There's a knock at the door and the Supervisor's Assistant scuttles in and whispers something in her ear. The Supervisor lets out an irritated sigh.

'I'm needed upstairs. Let me know when it's done.'

The door slams as she leaves.

There's a buzzing sound and I look up to see Guardian 12 shaving the sides of Arthur's head. It seems degrading. It makes him look smaller. More vulnerable. I want to make her stop, but I can't.

Guardian Rich catches my eye and then looks away.

The buzzing stops.

'I'll take it from here,' Guardian Rich says and then the other Guardians file out the room, job done. We're secured. Captive. Their force no longer needed. Next thing I know, Guardian Rich is pulling a screen around me and I can't see Arthur any more. My world is blue canvas. I can't even say goodbye.

The helmet starts to lower. It's tight round my head. Squeezing.

Then Guardian Rich is at my side again. There's a needle in my arm and he starts counting backwards from twenty.

The last sound I hear is fourteen.

ARTHUR

Hopeless. Useless. I couldn't even work a damned gun. I've failed her. I've failed the most amazing girl in the world. A numbness spreads over my body and invades my mind.

I would do anything to save her. Give anything.

The Guardian with the grey hair and round glasses emerges from behind the blue screens that surround Alba and then looks back at her hidden form curiously. His eyes are sad, his mouth sagging.

I don't understand. His attitude makes no sense.

And then it does. Maybe, just maybe…

I beckon him over, whispering so that no one might overhear us. I wouldn't be surprised if the place was bugged.

'Do you love her?' I ask.

'Yes,' he replies simply, looking almost relieved at being able to confess the truth.

'Then I have an idea.'

ALBA

At first there is nothing. A dark, silent void.

But then the blackness starts to recede and I begin to see colour – blue – and hear noises. A voice – soft, familiar.

Thoughts form in my head. Words, pictures. But then I remember. It's not me. They're not my thoughts. They belong to another brain; a brain that's now in my body. Arthur's.

So why does it feel like me?

It's like I'm still here. Still present. Perhaps this is how it happens. A trace of the former occupant remains, a ghost in the machine?

But I don't feel like a ghost. I test my recall, pulling up thought after thought. Curly. The Supervisor. Holding Arthur's hand. Being clamped down.

They don't feel like residual traces. They feel real. I send an instruction to my hand and my right thumb rotates slowly.

I'm still in control.

Something must have gone wrong with the procedure. A bubble of excitement builds. For some reason it didn't work. I'm still me. So Arthur must still be Arthur. We're special cases, somehow immune. Maybe they'll have to let us go.

'It went smoothly?' A harsher voice this time. The Supervisor's.

'Perfectly,' Guardian Rich replies.

What?

There's a jangling noise as the screen is pulled open, revealing the full extent of the Transition Room once more.

The seat opposite is empty. Arthur's gone. What have they done with him?

The Supervisor must have been watching my expression.

'Your previous body will be disposed of,' she says. 'We find clients find it too distressing to see it sitting there … empty.'

I choke back a sob. Arthur's body is lying on a metal trolley somewhere. Ready to be burnt. The arms that held me, the hand that wrapped around mine… And if his body's empty…

'I do hope there are no hard feelings, Mr, or should I say, Ms Easton?'

I don't reply, I'm still staring around the room, trying to work out what's happening. Why I still exist. My eyes alight on the computer in the middle. Guardian Rich is subtly reinserting a lead from my helmet back into the main device. Guardian Rich. He sabotaged it. He deliberately sabotaged it. He killed Arthur. Drained him instead of me. I know Arthur was dying anyway but still, he didn't have the right. It wasn't his choice to make. Where is Arthur now? What happens to a brain that's removed from a person but not downloaded into a new body? What *could* happen? He's gone. Gone forever.

Guardian Rich undoes the clasps and I stand. My legs collapse under me at first, but on the second attempt they hold my weight.

'If you'll follow me to my office, we'll complete the necessary paperwork,' the Supervisor instructs. 'I do hope you appreciate that we had your best interests at heart. We'll update your access codes with your new fingerprints. And you may wish to choose a new name.'

She opens the door and begins to strut down the corridor towards the lift. I follow her at a distance.

There's a scuffling sound and suddenly Guardian Rich is touching my elbow.

'You might want to read the note you left yourself,' he says. 'Clients often find waking up in a new body disorientating so they write themselves a note to calm and reassure themselves.'

I stare at him, confused.

'I believe you may have put it in this pocket.' He indicates to the pocket on the right of my tunic.

Gingerly I feel inside. He's right. There's a note. A piece of unlined white paper folded neatly in half. I open it, hands shaking.

I'd have recognised the handwriting anywhere. The loops. The slants. The flourish on the D. The way it chases itself off the page.

I begin to read.

Dearest Alba,

I am sorry it had to end this way. I promised I'd get you out and this is the only way I knew how. My only regret is that I didn't get to say goodbye.

I love you,

Your Arthur.

PS Find Tommy. You can trust him.

Tears streak down my face as I burrow the note back into my pocket. As I realise what he's done.

He sacrificed himself. For me. For love.

And I didn't even get to say goodbye.

Or tell him that I love him back.

I ride the lift in silence and stand, numb, as the Supervisor fills in forms and scans my fingerprint.

'Guardian 12 is going to fetch you some new, more appropriate clothing, which just leaves one more thing,' she says. 'Your new name. Any thoughts?'

I draw myself up to my full height and look her directly in the eye. She no longer frightens me. I feel like I finally exist now. And I'm going to make this existence count.

'Alba,' I say. 'My name is Alba.'

Also by the author:

THE TERRITORY
(a dystopian trilogy)

Noa Blake is just another normal 15 year old with exams looming. Except in The Territory normal isn't normal. The richest children have a node on the back of their necks and can download information, bypassing the need to study.

In a flooded world of dwindling resources, Noa and the other 'Norms' have their work cut out even to compete. And competing is everything – because everyone who fails the exams will be shipped off to the Wetlands, which means a life of misery, if not certain death.

But how to focus when your heart is being torn in two directions at once?

Winner of the TSBA 2018
'The 1984 of our time' the *Guardian* children's books
'A truly exceptional novel' *Booktrust*
'Thrilling and thought-provoking' *The Times*
'Gripping dystopia with a keen political edge' Imogen Russell Williams, *Metro*

INDIA SMYTHE STANDS UP

Fourteen-year-old India Smythe has caught the eye of Ennis, the hottest boy at St Joseph's. But nothing's ever easy when you're dealing with horrific teachers, a dad who's convinced every boy is a sex pest, a best friend who talks you into embarrassing makeovers to look good on Insta and the odd kissing-induced hospitalisation.
And does India even want Ennis?

Or should she risk social relegation and go for the orchestra geek with the extra-long forehead who she actually enjoys talking to?

'The new YA comedy teens need… when a book like *India Smythe Stands Up* comes along you need to get it into as many hands as possible' *Lucas Maxwell, BookRiot*

'One of the funniest protagonists since … well … ever! She fits in with Bridget Jones and Georgia Nicolson. The perfect antidote to the grim, grey times in which we find ourselves' *Teen Librarian*

Out now – the hilarious sequel,
INDIA SMYTHE IN LOVE?

Want to be the first to hear about
Sarah's upcoming books?

Join the mailing list through her website:
www.sarahgovett.com
Or follow her on Instagram/twitter @sarahgovett

Acknowledgments

Huge thanks as ever to my husband. Thanks to my agent, Jane Turnbull, for her boundless enthusiasm. Thanks to Earl, my incredible editor. Thanks to Liam Relph for the wonderful cover – I love it! Thanks to Kirsty Ridge for her eagle-eyed proof reading. And, finally, thanks to my children for giving me the space to write. Well, sort of.

Sarah Govett graduated with a First in Law from Trinity College, Oxford. After qualifying as a solicitor she set up her own tutoring agency before turning her energies to writing. Her first trilogy, *The Territory*, won the Trinity Schools Book Award and the Gateshead Teen Book Award and was described by the *Guardian* Children's Books site as 'the 1984 of our time'. It has now been optioned for TV.

Sarah is an in-demand speaker at secondary schools and has appeared at the Southbank Literature Festival, the Edinburgh International Book Festival, the Bradford Literature Festival and the Godolphin Literature Festival.

She lives in London with her husband and three young children.